SOUL COLLECTOR PROPHECY

DYSFUNCTION AT ITS FINEST BOOK 2

J.M. DABNEY

HOSTILE WHISPERS PRESS, LLC

PROLOGUE

AMORA MEDINA-JACKYL

rutality and blood stained the Jackyl lineage. Amora proved herself the cruelest, yet there were brighter times before she'd become a killer. Memories existed in the dark recesses of her mind cloaked by her torture at the hands of a Dark Age cult and the subsequent body count left in the existence of her four centuries.

Sanity wasn't her strong suit. That was precisely the reason she once more stood outside the chamber that led to Dominic. The Jumper was almost as crazy as her. She couldn't blame him, though. Trapped inside essentially a rotting sarcophagus, he moved from one skin suit to the next. Except for this time, a mutual enemy turned Dominic's latest body into his future coffin. The bastard spoke in riddles, and half of what came out of his thin, wrinkled lips was bullshit half-truths. She needed answers, and he was her only option.

"Amora, are you sure you want to do this," her companion asked.

She glanced to her left and quickly assessed the concern in Morgana's eyes. Being unable to dematerialize and reconfigure left her with a need for a lift of sorts. "I don't have a choice here."

"There's always a choice, Amora."

She barely restrained the urge to roll her eyes. "Is there and where is your choice," she sarcastically asked The Untouchable.

Morgana was a rare breed; most of her kind didn't make it out of their teens. The suicide rate was astounding. Morgana healed by taking the pain and injuries of others. Some saw death and destruction, or remote viewers who could only live their lives through others. Prized for their curses—kept as pets. Prisoners of Fate's making.

"It's to help where I'm able. Mine was a painful decision, but what I do helps a lot of people."

"By you taking on another's injury, another's pain for nothing more than a thanks."

"I do what needs done, but seeking this demon's help isn't necessary or even prudent." Morgana chided and lifted her little, pointed nose in the air.

"What about being a Jackyl has ever turned out to be prudent?" Amora could list on one hand the times she'd taken the safe way out. Safe wasn't in her vocabulary; nothing ever happened if people took the easy way.

"That is true. Should I leave you to your task and return later?"

"No, I'll meet you at the extraction point." She didn't want Morgana too close to the action. The woman could heal others, but she was useless in a fight.

"Very well, I do hope to see you again."

"Thanks for the vote of confidence."

"You're most welcome." Morgana's body shimmered into a hazy outline until it disappeared altogether. Teleportation was rare among species other than demons, angels and the like. Lucky for Amora, Morgana was willing to help, if a bit reluctant.

She reached out and swept aside the thick tapestry to push open the concealed door. The faint scents of decay and sulfur greeted her, then the smell of smoke from a wood fire in a stone fireplace.

"Warrior Jackyl, such a pleasure." A black-cloaked figure hobbled out of the shadows. Bones audibly creaked, and once again she wondered about the expiration date on the meat suit.

"Dominic." She ignored the title, stepped inside, but kept the door cracked behind her. The chamber was spacious enough, but the windowless room was too much like the cell she'd lived in for decades.

"What brings you here alone? Shouldn't your second-in-command be glaring at me from just over your right shoulder?"

"Are you going to pretend stupidity?" Amora stepped to the side and put her back to the wall. She'd sense anyone before they'd get close, yet old habits were impossible to break. She folded her arms over her chest and let the silence lengthen as she waited out the ancient demon.

"We've discussed you ruining my limited amusement, Amora."

"Yeah, yeah, do I have to ask the fucking questions?" Amora wasn't in the mood for Dominic's games, but she'd anticipated it. The demon wasn't free with the information even on days he felt generous.

"Impatience, a rather annoying flaw."

"I know I'm ruining your fun. Repetitiveness is beneath you, demon, so just cut the shit and get on with it."

"Our future Collector still languishes on his Sabbatical. His physical pursuits of mortal pleasure grow tiresome. It's a waste of his purpose."

"So instead of fucking his way through countless women, he should resign himself to banishing your jailer. You're going to tell me his ascension wouldn't benefit you, maybe grant you freedom."

"I will admit no such thing. My motives are far from noble. Angelus Kali, he's your real purpose for visiting. You know I can't—"

"You mean won't give me the information I need. Dominic, cut the bullshit. My son's fate is sealed, his choices taken from him and there's not a fucking thing I can do for him. Although, you're more than capable of telling me some version of the truth in your roundabout way."

"What is it you seek, Amora?"

"The reason my parents were murdered."

"It was more of an assassination. The aligning of Medina and Jackyl warriors threatened the dictatorship of The Council. As you've worked for them, you know of their penchant for the brutal enforcement of their laws. How far will you go for your answers?"

"Short of selling my soul—sorry, I lost that a long time ago. What else do you want for the answers?"

"Open your mind, Warrior Jackyl, and I'll allow you this one moment of absolute truth. I'll accept my punishment from my despised Master. It can't be any worse than living inside a rotting corpse which in exactly a few years' time will be what will happen to me."

"Is today a good day to die?"

"Not for you, Amora. I still have use of you."

"And what happens when I'm no longer useful?"

"That day hasn't come—soon, but not yet."

She wasn't an idiot and knew her time ran out quicker than she wanted. "What do you want?"

"Just close your eyes." His voice transitioned from weak to the inhuman growl of the creature inside.

Today is a good day to die, Amora silently said to herself. Secure that her mate and their daughter were provided for—that she kept her promise of never vowing to come home—she flexed her fingers around her biceps and let her eyes drift close.

"Be careful what you wish for, Warrior, some secrets were never meant to come to light."

The flare of agony exploded inside her head, and she wasn't inside Dominic's prison.

* * *

Mud squelched under the soles of leather boots. Cold armor weighted her body down and screams echoed from every direction. Her fingers tightened around the thick hilt of her sword. The ground wasn't wet from rain, but blood from bodies collapsed in every direction. Hooves pounded the earth as the battalion of knights on horseback approached, bearing down on her from all sides.

"Mistress Medina," a weathered faced Knight with battle-dented armor called out. She sheathed her sword. "No one remains. The bastards fled. We have knights in pursuit, what say you?"

She surveyed the scene. Men, women, and children in grotesque carica-
ture impaled upon pikes. The wooden lances exited through mouths and the
tops of skulls. "Lay them all to rest," the voice wasn't hers. Pain and sadness
filled it, but Amora had shielded those emotions centuries ago.

"All, Mistress?"

"Yes, all. They went to battle for us, so we will give them their due
respect."

"As you wish." The knight bowed and turned his mount away and issued
orders as he disappeared.

She wasn't in her body. Did she see the past through her mother's eyes?
Metal clanked as she moved deeper into the carnage. The wariness of battle
weighted her limbs. She was tired. It was a soul-deep exhaustion of too many
battles fought with no end in sight. Amora reached up, removed her helmet
and dropped to her knees in front of a group of impaled corpses. Depression
she'd remembered from the night The Order of Angelus killed her family took
over her being. She lifted her hand and extended it towards the bare, bloody
feet of a woman maybe in her late thirties. Just as she almost touched the cold
skin, it disappeared, and fog surrounded her. Amora couldn't see more than
six feet in front of her.

"This place isn't for you, child." The thick, damp fog parted, and a woman
stepped forward. She was dressed in the same uniform as Amora moments
before.

"I haven't been a child for a very long time."

"I know this. You may have believed yourself alone, but someone was
always there."

"Who are you and what do you know about me being alone?"

"I'm Mistress Arian Medina of the Medina Warriors, your grandmother.
You shouldn't have made that deal with Dominic. What you learn here can't
be of help."

"What happened?"

"The Council has forgotten its place. What they will not give us, we take
by force."

"So the Council, the so-called benevolent rulers of our combined species,'
murdered all those people?"

"Those people were our coven—our family—even if we didn't share blood *or of the same species; they were still ours. Does that change your opinion of the Council?"*

"I'm not concerned about the Council. What I want to know is what the fuck I'm supposed to do about Kali?"

"Angelus still a nuisance? He's a babe throwing a tantrum over being denied a teat."

"He does love his childish outbursts."

"You didn't help anything by siring his next in line. You and Demonus sure, how do you say, fucked up?"

"True, but to keep my family safe, what do I have to do?"

"What you already do, trust no one. Keep your back to the wall and strike down anyone that believes the heir to the Medina-Jackyl Warriors can't destroy anyone in her wake. Amora, things are going to become even worse."

"We don't leave family behind, Arian."

"No, we don't, never have and never will. I do have a bit of advice, Amora."

"Oh, and what's that?"

"You have more enemies than even you realize. Treat the Council and Kali with the same degree of disdain and distrust. When given the chance, destroy them all. Time to go, Amora. Be safe, don't let my daughter and her mate's lost lives be in vain. Rebuild our family and then—"

"Then what?"

"Kill all our enemies and display them as a warning to the next genera-tion just as Kali and the Council displayed our coven as a caveat for us. Leave no one left to breed." Arian and her voice faded back into the mist.

The pain detonated in her head again and everything went black.

* * *

BLOOD DRIED on her skin and caked thick and dark under her nails. Her arrival at the extraction point hadn't been smooth. What were a few more bodies? If what happened to her—meeting a long-dead ancestor was true, then she was supposed to kill them all. Not that she needed permission. There wasn't anything wrong with doing what someone was good at.

Amora's wounds healed, but not quickly enough. She needed to feed, and for that she required Lark. She closed the door to block out the rising sun. It was always another battle. *I'm too old for this shit.* But there was no way in hell she would admit it to anyone. She was also tired of living with a target on her back, but it had been that way longer than she could remember.

She scanned her loft checking for signs of danger. The panic room door stood open, and she silently strode towards it. She crossed her arms and leaned against the doorjamb. Her wife stood in front of the easel studying the canvas.

"Can you ever come home not covered in blood and who knows what else," Lark asked without turning around.

"You haven't even turned around. How can you tell I'm bloody?" Amora smirked at Lark's little, exasperated huff.

"We've been married long enough."

"A year is long enough? You already thinking about divorce?"

Lark spun and glared at her. "You know what I mean, Amora."

"You get all sexy when you're irritated with me. C'mere."

"Not until you wash off whatever that is." Lark motioned towards her clothes.

Amora glanced down to find mystery chunks on her black t-shirt. "We're like an old married couple now."

"What's wrong? You've been quiet recently. Not unusual for you, but it happens a lot when you're thinking."

She didn't know how to explain what was going on or what happened. When she was able to wrap her head around what occurred, she'd tell Lark about her projection to another realm. "Ripper, he needs to get his head out of his ass and get to work."

"We discussed this. Ripper needs time. We're always living on high alert. What he craves is warring with his misguided sense of chivalry and nothing you do or say can change that. Especially not bullying him into doing what you want." Lark chuckled. "He's immune to that."

"I could just kick his ass for being a moron. What's so hard about coming home and doing what you're supposed to? He's running, and Jackyl's don't run. It's embarrassing."

"Amora."

Her wife's voice turned cold with warning, and Amora shook her head. Who knew the honeymoon would be over after a year? They still had a few centuries or more to go, unless an enemy cut that short.

"Don't Amora me. Fuck, he's got a mate—a family—here, and he insists on trying to do the fucking noble thing." There was that word again: noble. The anti-heroines/heroes didn't do noble. Her reputation was going to fall to ruin if it got out that a Medina-Jackyl possessed such a weakness.

"You don't have to say it like *noble* is a disgusting word. When it's time, and he's ready, that's when he'll stop running."

"See? Even you think he's running. Kali is going to take advantage of this weakness."

"Love isn't a weakness." She understood Ripper's need for time and patience. Neither of which they had the privilege of possessing.

"I didn't say it was a weakness." Lark was turning her words around and taking them out of context.

"You implied it."

"Are we fighting?"

"No, fighting ends in makeup sex, and it's not happening."

"It could."

"No, now, back to the problem at hand. What are your concerns?"

"Are we playing psychologist and patient again? I don't like that game."

"Don't make me laugh; we're being serious now."

"Fine, Kali keeps trying to kill what's mine, my mate, and children. We don't have time for Ripper's soul-searching. It's time for battle plans and body count."

"Aw, there is the vicious vamp that I know and love," Lark stopped inches away from her. "You need a shower. Did you take on an army?"

"Only fifteen or so, but maybe more. I wasn't counting." Lark huffed, and Amora repressed a chuckle. It would earn her a glare and threat of a night on the couch, but she'd never actually slept away from Lark unless Amora was on a mission.

"Did Dominic give you what you needed?"

"When does he?"

"Okay, stupid question. Come on, love. I'll wash your back, and you can go all Alpha as a reward for a battle won. Isn't that what the Ladies did for their knights coming home from crusades?"

"What do you know of knights?" Amora asked as she reached out and grabbed Lark's hands to tug her towards the bathroom.

"I'm guilty of a weakness for cheesy romances when I'm waiting for my wife to come home."

"Then welcome your warrior home. I've missed you."

Amora pushed away the troubles to come and took her wife to the shower. Soon enough they'd once again be back to back on the battlefield. Amora reserved the little bit of softness she possessed for her wife. First, she'd love on her wife and afterward she'd form a plan. She'd found her place of peace. She just hoped her son would find his as well.

CHAPTER 1

*I*ncense smoke hung in the air like a cloud, spice and musk and Ripper watched the shifting of it above him. Candle-light flickered in the cloudy haze; the subtle chaos pulled him in, and he became lost in thought. Soft fingertips stroked his skin in teasing circles. The temporary oblivion he found in the stranger's body didn't ease the maelstrom of regret.

He'd lost himself in countless females in his nearly two centuries, but he wanted more, a particular form. Only one female would do, his demon begged for her, and he couldn't allow himself to acquiesce. Lying with a monster would be too much to ask of the woman.

Grumbling flowed from deep in his chest and a feminine hand wrapped around his dick, he dislodged it and rolled from bed. "Time to go," he called over his shoulder as he walked towards the dresser and grabbed his phone off the top. He scrolled through the contacts until he found the number he was looking for and tapped the screen to connect the call.

"Yeah?" He smiled at the annoyed sound of Amora's voice. His mother wasn't the most pleasant woman.

"You and Jailbait mind having company?" He knew calling Lark jailbait would get a rise out of the vamp.

"Quit calling my mate that. Is it time?"

The cryptic question didn't need clarification.

"Yes, Ma, I'm coming home." He was still reticent about returning home. With the decision came the knowledge he wouldn't be able to avoid Tasha. The time Ripper took for himself was selfish, and now he needed to get home to take care of his promise to Amora.

"We'll see you soon. Don't wake Meadow up when you appear."

The call disconnected, and he grinned. His mother being all maternal and shit with her mate's baby sister was amusing. Amora's reputation didn't mesh with the new, slightly softer vamp, and by slightly softer he meant she didn't try to kill everyone she met.

Ripper set his phone back on the surface, and he turned and dragged his fingers through his hair. "I don't care if you ain't going home, but it's time to get your ass moving." He walked to the bed and slapped the woman's exposed ass; she squealed and instantly glared at him.

"Asshole!"

"You're wasting time. In a few minutes, I'll walk your ass naked out the door." His voice must have shown how serious he was because she double-timed it, picking up her clothes and dressing as she hopped on one foot then the other to the door.

His tense muscles instantly relaxed as the door closed behind the strange, nameless woman and he looked around the cheap Paris flat. There wasn't much to pack–he traveled as light as possible. Too many possessions or people weighed him down, but it was time to go home. The torture would begin; to be so close to his mate and never able to possess her would slowly kill him. His demon screamed for her, demanded that he claim what was his, yet what could he offer Tasha? A life with a monster destined to survive only by means of collecting souls to feed the hunger that grew intense by staggering degrees every day. He would ascend his grandfather's throne, take his rightful place and where did that leave him with his mate?

Tasha knew what Amora was, but only knew one side of him. If he claimed her, he would have to reveal the demon half of himself. It would all have to be laid on the line.

He didn't know if he could open himself to her rejection. Tasha treated him as a kid, Amora's flirty son, but she didn't see or understand that he'd walked this world for nearly two hundred years. She only saw what was on the surface, the man appearing only in his mid-twenties, and she was a woman of thirty-five. The lush, ample curves and the fall of black hair that fell to the flares of her hips, he craved her. It wasn't only want, a momentary slacking of lust, no, she was his in every way, except one.

All he had to do was have faith, take that leap into the unknown and finally accept the darkness and light of his fate. His gut clenched as pain seared through his center, it nearly took him off his feet, and he caught himself by bracing his palm on the nightstand. The time wasn't right, he wasn't ready, just a little longer, he could take the pain and anything else his demon wanted to throw at him. He wouldn't submit until death was his only other option.

Ripper stretched out on the bed and crossed his arms under his head. All he had were fantasies and dreams, and sometimes they lessened his discontent and others they were torture. He'd denied his mate for her safety, but moments when he was alone he'd indulged— let himself imagine the perfection of his Tasha. Ripper let out a long sigh and lost himself in a short respite. His lids lazily fell as the female from earlier faded, and another took her place in the forefront of his mind.

Skin the shade of sweet cream spread across the midnight blue of his sheets. Full, ample curves on full display, exposed for him and only him and he hissed as he crouched over her covering her form with his own. She wore a teasing crooked grin as she raised her arms and reached for him. The heat and need in her eyes drew him in; humbled by her desire for the monster he was beneath the tanned human flesh. A demon is rippling under the tight rein begging for release, to claim.

"Ripper." Her whisper was low and husky as she twined her fingers around the nape of his neck to pull him down. He shivered as his chest connected with hers and hard, swollen nipples branded his chest. Hesitating on the edge, building the anticipation as their lips barely met letting their breaths mingle. Pressure formed in his eyes as he felt them shift, he knew they

were glowing green, and the pupils had turned into thin, slender vertical slashes. He froze waiting for her inevitable retreat and screams of horror. The only reaction was the shifting of her mouth below his before her plump lips met his.

Her fleshy thighs and shapely calves twined around his waist, "Do it. Don't make me wait!"

The demand was the only insistence he needed, he reached around under her thigh, and he wrapped his hand around the base of his cock. He lost all control as he felt the slick heat on the head of his dick, and with a great roar, he slammed forward. "Yes!" she screamed as her nails scored his back, the pain pushing him further beyond his restraint.

Piston snaps of his hips, sweaty skin slapped together vulgarly, and he rode her with years of pent-up need. She squeaked, grunted and demanded harder, faster. Her large breasts rubbed against his chest and thighs gripped his sides.

"Fuck! Can you take harder?"

A nod was the only answer he needed, and he rutted against her, the demon beneath the surface rippling forth. His skin was shifting from hair-roughened tan to smooth serpent. He forced it away, deeper, as he watched her lift her arms to brace her palms against the headboard.

His mate was beautiful beyond measure, and the brutal taking of her body caused her breasts to bounce wildly, her softly curved stomach quivered. Tasha's pussy rippled around his cock with a vice-like grip.

"Gods, faster, fuck me, fuck me!"

He ripped away from her and turned her onto her knees. She wrapped her hands around the back of the bed, and he slammed home once more. Screams and pleas urged him on, sweat ran down his skin and his needle-like fangs dragged over her damp nape.

With each thrust she slammed back, meeting him with surprising strength. Ripper straightened and curved his hands over her shoulders. The wet sex sounds filled the room, joining the symphony of moans, grunts, and her high-pitched squeaks. Patches of smooth black scales appeared, shimmering, there one moment, gone the next.

"Mine, no one else's." His tone dark and demanding, he staked his claim *as clearly as his cock disappearing into her pretty, swollen cunt. The angle of his hips changed, and she arched, her head thrown back as she froze.*

The hot gush flowed from her, down their thighs and soaked the bed—he never slowed. He showed no mercy, he took and demanded as she clawed at the wall. "To—too much, no more." He refused to let her free, he rammed harder and faster, her body jerking and her pleas frantic and frightened. He covered her body, and his mouth found her ear.

"You will cum again and again until I'm satisfied. Mine, I own you!" He roared as he pushed her towards another orgasm, one after another, his body on fire, his muscles corded and stood out beneath human and serpent skin. Ripper's hair stuck to his face, and he used her body. She pleaded for more, and in nearly the same breath, begged him to stop. They melded into one. His hands covered her breasts as he plucked roughly at her nipples, tugged and twisted as she bucked trying to get away.

"Ripper, too much, so fucking..." A keening cry and he pushed through the resistance of her abused pussy. The heat built in his lower back and his abs contracted as his sac drew up tight. "Fuck me, cum, fill me!" His fangs pierced her skin, held firm as his body bowed and he emptied deep into her welcoming body.

THE SOUND of shredding fabric forced his eyes open. Claw marks ruined the bed sheets, and the bitter taste of venom filled his mouth. His serpent was too close to the surface. He'd only lost control of his demon once before, and he remembered the days locked inside himself while it hunted. Ripper tightened his abs and rolled to a sitting position, ignoring his hard cock.

He set his elbows on his knees and rested his head in his hands. It was time to go home, face his mate, and exist with the knowledge he could never touch. Fantasies were poor substitutes, but not being around her at all would be worse.

CHAPTER 2

lub Revenge. Tasha Cisco couldn't imagine being anywhere else. She hadn't exactly seen herself as a Burlesque performer ten years after her first step onto that stage. Her co-workers and boss were the family she'd always wanted. Her biological family barely acknowledged her existence except at holidays when attendance was mandatory. Everything was perfect. Tasha was right where she wanted to be, but only one thing dampened her contentment. She needed to get laid.

Tasha's sex drive went through the roof a year ago, and she hadn't received one invite or date since. She'd had her share of one-night stands, but she tended to steer clear of relationships. Permanence made her jumpy.

"Do I need to lose weight?" Tasha Cisco sighed as she laid her upper body on the bar and whined to her boss, Amora Medina-Jackyl. She was filling out more with each day she barreled closer to middle age. Okay, thirty-five wasn't that close to middle age, but still, she wasn't twenty-five anymore.

"Tasha, darlin', you don't need to lose an ounce, you're my top performer. I'd prefer if you didn't."

Of course Amora would say that. The vamp had a weakness for curves and softness, if the woman's mate was any indication.

"Then why can't I get laid, Big Boss? You'd fuck me, right?" She turned her head when someone snickered, and Tasha scrunched her nose at Amora's mate, Lark. "Sorry, Lark." The woman was innocent in appearance, but a force to be reckoned with, she had to be as she was Amora's mate.

"No need to be. My woman is quite popular and exceptionally talented. Amora, love, would you do our Tasha?"

Amora's chuckle made her face heat. "In a heartbeat, if I technically had one that wasn't for show."

"Ha, ha, you two are not funny. It's been a year since anyone has shown any interest. A year, Amora!"

"That's bullshit, what about—"

Tasha lifted a brow as her boss stopped speaking and attempted to think of someone.

"Yeah, not one person sniffing around."

"Don't have many people as patrons here. What about a human club or bar? Maybe your luck will be better. It is common knowledge I don't allow anyone to fuck with my employees."

"When I'm not here, I'm at home sleeping, and what's wrong with non-humans? They don't like a woman with a little cushion?"

It hadn't been long after she started working at Revenge that she'd noticed things weren't as they seemed. Those creatures in horror movies and all those paranormal romances existed in one fashion or another. Tasha had to admit that she'd panicked for about a week and showed back up to work. She loved her badass boss, fangs, blood-imbibing and all.

"You're beautiful, Tasha. Amora's right, you don't need to change. Why don't you take a night off and get away from here?" Lark's suggestion sounded great, but she was just fucked and not in a good way.

"My mate is right, take off tomorrow night and your usual night, it will give you two days off back to back. Rest one and go out the other. Find a beautiful piece to curl your toes."

"Are you sure?" As a performer, bartender and part-time manager she didn't have a lot of free time. If she wasn't working, Tasha didn't know what to do with herself.

"I've semi-retired from my second career, so you can take a few days off for yourself, Tasha. It'll do you good, Darlin'."

"It would be nice to find an actual date maybe, not that I wouldn't say no to a good hard fuck."

The atmosphere thickened, heat shifted beneath her skin, and she didn't even have to look to know who suddenly appeared behind her. His steps were always silent or whispers of sound. Ripper was a torturous temptation walking for mere mortals such as herself. Another reason her life wasn't all sunshine and roses stood behind her. He wasn't even close to her, and she could still—feel him.

"Anyone in particular?"

The warm whiskey smooth rumble abruptly made her pussy clench, and her body screamed for a pounding she'd feel for days' fuck. She moaned as her eyes rolled upward and Amora cleared her throat.

"We were telling Tasha she should walk on the dark side and hit a human bar. Lark could go with you…she hasn't had a night to herself in months."

"Thank you, love, but why would I need a night to myself when my sexy mate is so readily available?"

Tasha laughed at the teasing edge of Lark's question, and Amora groaned. Tasha turned her head and caught Lark holding Ripper's scruffy cheeks.

"Good to have you home, I missed my baby boy." She snorted as the young woman pinched her grown, stepson's cheeks and he just smiled at her indulgently.

"I love you too, Mom." Ripper twined his arms around Lark and lifted her off her feet.

"Took you long enough to show up."

Her lips twitched at Amora's annoyed tone. Mother and son were barely civil when they were in the same room, although she knew it was all a show. She found it amusing as hell.

"The warm welcome is overwhelming." Ripper's voice was thick with sarcasm.

"If you wanted a warm welcome you should've been home months ago. I'm getting tired of your shit."

"Missed me, Ma?"

"Like a case of the Clap."

"As eloquent as ever."

Ripper snorted and turned his attention to her. She scarcely resisted the impulse to retreat slowly, then make a run for it.

"Tasha, you're thinking of dating a human? Why would you go slumming when you already got the perfect man?"

"Baby Boss, I don't need to be looking like some Cougar robbing the cradle, but thanks for the offer, honey." She reached out and patted his arm, the softness of his features changed, hardened and drove away the always mischievous expression he wore. She jerked back, turned away and met Amora's gaze.

"I'll take those days off. Maybe I just need a spa day." An eerie chill worked its way down her spine, and she couldn't ignore the tangible glare of Ripper's striking green eyes with the yellow starburst around the pupils. "Okay, boss, this isn't getting me anywhere. Meadow," Tasha called for the little girl.

Tiny tennis shoes squeaked over the dance floor as Lark's baby sister appeared from her hiding spot under the stage. "You ready to dance?"

"Yay!" Tasha hopped down from the stool and scooped the pint-sized toddler under her arm. "Momma 'Mora, I gon' dance!"

"Yes, you are. Tasha, don't encourage my girl too much, I prefer she not grace my stage one day."

"Something wrong with being a performer, Amora?"

"I barely stay on the right-ish side of the law now."

Tasha raised a brow at Amora's right-ish comment and waited.

"Okay, nowhere near law-abiding. But Meadow getting touched by some drunk—" Amora's hands clenched so tight the knuckles cracked.

"Aw, you're so—maternal."

"Fuck off, and get to practicing. Can't have you embarrassing me in front of a full house."

"Never!" She smiled sweetly at Amora and ran for the stage with the girl wildly giggling.

Her practice music began as she stepped onto the stage, and she set Meadow down and picked up the large, black feather fans. On stage is where she lost herself, doubt and insecurity didn't exist. Simply her and the music, the audience always on the peripheral and today she needed the escape. Tasha ignored the fact that others watched and just danced.

* * *

TASHA'S SWEAT-DAMPENED skin glistened under the heat of the spot-lights, and she ended her practice by laying her fans aside. The soft tips tickled over her arms and she smiled. Typically she was focused, but she'd been distracted by the heated conversation at the bar between Ripper and Amora—which wasn't unusual. Those two loved to fight.

Bloodshed wasn't an uncommon occurrence when those two butted heads. Their last big fight instigated a betting war with Amora as the favorite and Ripper was pissed. It had made him sloppy, and she'd lost two hundred dollars. She'd given him shit for months about that. That happened not long before their friendship turned south, but she still didn't understand why it went awkward.

Ripper was beautiful like a male model. His dark blond hair was a bit long touching his collar in the back and falling into his eyes in front. Stubble a few shades darker than his hair covered his lean jaw and cheeks. Ripper held a leanly built frame, yet corded with muscle. He was the type of guy she'd lusted after in high school and college. The kind who never gave her a second glance. Ripper made her feel like she was still that nerdy, chunky girl she'd thought she'd left behind.

She darted a look at Meadow to see her playing with the mini-fans she'd had specially made for her. Two days a week she took the little girl to ballet while Amora slept and Lark took care of office work. It was amazing the change in the child in the past year. Meadow arrived a somewhat happy, but sullen child, preferring her own company. There was more laughter and smiles these days, and the little girl brightened the lives of the family of Club Revenge.

"Beautiful as always, Tasha." Ripper's voice startled her making her jump slightly.

"Th—thanks." She took the bottle of water offered and nearly whined as he sat down on the stage close to her. "Amora mentioned you're moving home." He leaned against her and pushed her gently with his shoulder. Ripper always smelled so good, spicy and masculine.

"Temporarily. Those two go at it like monkeys on speed. I don't need to be scarred further."

She chuckled and shook her head. "I didn't think you liked it here." She glanced toward Meadow to find her twirling the fans with a big smile. Tasha looked back at Ripper.

"Not particularly, but moving back has its benefits." Her chest tightened as his eyes traveled slowly over her.

"Oh, what might those be?"

"Beignets."

Tasha chuckled at the longing in his tone. She remembered the last time he was home he'd eaten himself sick. "You have to be careful of the dangers of human food." The tension eased a bit as the natural camaraderie resurfaced. They'd been friends for a long time even through the sexual tension, even if it was one-sided. She used to wish she could take his flirting and innuendo seriously, but she knew it would only lead to heartbreak.

"I'll chance it." The soft smile on his face dropped as he stared into her eyes. "Don't go on this hunt for a date. We both know what you want." She forced her body not to flinch as he tucked his face against her neck. His breath hot against the side of her throat threatened to make her eyes roll.

"Ripper, we've—" His fingertips skimmed the bare curve of her thigh, and then slipped under the fabric of her short cutoffs.

"You almost came when you heard my voice."

Tasha wished she could deny it. Her need for Ripper tortured her for years, but she tried so long to hide it. She trembled, and air shuddered passed her lips at the intense pleasure of his fingers caressing lightly along her thigh. Tasha gasped at the strange tickling of his tongue on her throat.

"I bet you love it hard and fast, riding the line between pleasure and pain." His voice slowed to an odd hiss, she looked at him, and all mental function ceased as an elongated, black bifurcated tongue slithered from between his lips. Reality slammed her back to the present, and she tried to pull away.

"What—um, I have to go—shower."

"Need company?"

She almost answered yes as her thighs clenched as he repeated that rapid flicking thing. What would that feel like on her nipples and between her legs?

"Stop that," Tasha blurted out. She stood with every intention of fleeing, but a strong arm barred her escape. Ripper stepped in close positioning himself beside and slightly in front of her.

"I've waited far too long to have you." He tenderly stroked her cheek and urged her eyes to meet his. "You're mine, have been from the moment I met you. Tomorrow, I'll come—" She cut him off there.

His arrogance irritated her, and she'd shut him down now. No way was she going to be one more in a long line. Neither her heart nor confidence could take it.

"No, you won't, I know you, Ripper." She gathered all the strength and willpower she possessed. "You'll fuck anything that bats their lashes at you. You forget, I've known you for nearly a decade, and I may be a big girl, a thick chick, but I sure as hell won't be another notch for the Great Ripper Jackyl."

"Tasha."

She ignored him calling her name as she pulled away and grabbed her bag. Each footfall was ripping at her gut. She'd stupidly fallen in love with him. Making that mistake was enough, she wouldn't compound it further by being just another of his playthings. She waved at a concerned Lark and a pissed off Amora. She didn't need the questions. Tasha stepped outside and deeply inhaled, then slowly exhaled as she attempted to get her body under control.

Tasha had a feeling her boss knew of Tasha's predicament—of her feelings for Ripper, but thankfully Amora never said anything. It was hard enough to deal with it without everyone cracking jokes as was their habit or regarding her with even a trace of pity. She turned and headed toward the heavenly scent of coffee. Caffeine and maybe chocolate, they always made her feel better.

CHAPTER 3

*F*ucking up should be something he'd grown used to by now. He hadn't meant to come on to Tasha as intense as he had. Hell, he hadn't intended to do it at all.

That was why he avoided home. Just being in the same room with her and his demon won and attempted to get what it—they needed. He'd weighed the pros and cons, and the latter won out. His life and future were too dangerous for Tasha.

What would happen if she ever saw what he was? He'd hidden that side from her the entire length of their friendship. The scales, the needle-like venomous fangs, and the twelve-foot serpent/humanoid form. He couldn't let her see it.

Ripper stared intensely into his mug of blood as Amora slept, and Lark cuddled on the couch with her sister. His mother hadn't turned her mate yet, believing Meadow needed to live in the sun and Lark needed to remain mortal longer. The two made an odd pair. Lark was the epitome of fresh-faced innocence and Amora, well, she was a killer through and through. His mother never hesitated over a kill or second-guessed her actions. Except Lark and Meadow had shaved down the hardened edges—curbed her homicidal tendencies.

"Don't waste your breakfast." Lark admonished from across the room.

"Yes, Mom." He smiled at Lark as she slowly strode towards him.

"Don't be a smartass."

"Such language, Ma has indeed corrupted you."

"You're so funny, Ripper, but your jokes are less distracting than your mother's. She's better at it than you."

"You have me all figured out." He sarcastically admitted.

"What has you so troubled?" She leaned her forearms on the counter and stared up at him with her big blue eyes all soft and loving. Ripper wondered if Lark was what a real mom was like. Amora was homicidal and twisted, but loving and tender weren't how anyone who met Amora would describe the vamp.

Although, it amused him the woman who was almost two hundred years younger than him looked at as if he were her son. To be honest, he enjoyed Lark's maternal instincts because Amora wasn't the motherly type. The vamp loved him, he knew she did, but something inside his mother broke during the decades of torture at the hands of The Order. Lark seemed determined to make up for it. It's why he'd quickly come to love her as what she was—his mother.

"Do I have to say?" Distraction attempt number two, she squinted at him, and he admitted defeat.

"Answering a question with a question, Ripper, the solution is simple."

"It's not simple, I have to ascend one day, and I've no other choice. The pain will tear me apart." The pain was already there. The connection to his mate would lessen it to some degree, but it wouldn't completely go away until he accepted his fate.

"This is your birthright, Ripper, you are not Angelus, not cruel or arrogant. Look on this as a gift, one which you can do with as you see fit. Become Angelus, or run the Kali Empire the way you want."

"What if I can choose only one, Tasha or the title?" It was his biggest fear that he would claim Tasha and then have to give her up when the fated day came.

"Ripper, I love you, but you've set your sights a bit high with our Tasha."

"Ouch, Mom." He grabbed his chest. "Thanks." He scowled as Lark giggled.

"You're welcome. Men always want what they can't have."

Lark has been around Amora too long. His Ma was souring Lark's sweetness. "You need to get a new wife."

"I love the woman I have. We're talking about Tasha being too good for you. You can never have her."

Reverse psychology wouldn't work on him, but he'd play into it just to make her smile. "Oh, I could have her."

"You may have reached nearly two hundred years, yet this baby face—" He glared as she pinched his cheeks. "Doesn't show it, knowing what you are and seeing you are two different things. Tasha sees you as too young, and she has some—" He snarled to cut her off.

"I heard some of the conversation. She...I know what she thinks, and not all of it has to do with my age. Tasha doesn't think I'm serious."

"Have you tried explaining she's your mate, destined for you? Or that you've imprinted on her so no male of non-human origin will even dare touch her?"

"How did you know that? Is that why y'all tried to talk her into the human club?" They'd endeavored to betray him, one day they'd pay for that one.

"You can't do that to her. It isn't fair. You're manipulative. Tasha, the very voluptuous and sexy Tasha, performs nearly nude and sometimes nude on stage most nights and doesn't get hit on. That wasn't very subtle, and your mother annoyingly approves."

"Of course she would." He sighed. "Mom, it's not that easy. I don't want her to see what I truly am."

"Actually, you in your real form is rather spectacular."

"You only think that because you're weird and my stepmom. You're supposed to adore me."

"Yes, those are true, but, no, I think you're beautiful because you are. That gorgeous onyx skin with hints of emerald. A fine form, not as elegant as your mother—"

"And you can stop right there."

Lark laughed and shook her head. "You're too easy."

"That's what Tasha thinks too."

"I watched your approach yesterday, it left much to be desired, Son."

"I've waited so long though. It's like a war is waging between my selfishness that wants to take her and the honorable side which wants to protect her from an eternity with me."

"Angelus is unfortunately not yet dead, so you still have time before you have to take his place. You need to prove to Tasha you're actually worthy of being her mate."

"And how do I do that?"

"Woo her, Ripper, sweep her off her feet, and the rest will work itself out."

"Yes, oh wise one."

"You remind me too much of my Amora sometimes."

"Why must you bust my balls like that?"

"Stop, I love your mother and also you, now, have your breakfast."

Ripper smiled when Lark kissed his cheek and hugged him tightly, then returned to Meadow. Unaccustomed to jealousy, he didn't know how to handle the envy he felt. Amora found her mate after four hundred years and an astronomical body count, yet he couldn't even get his to give him a chance.

He wanted to claim, to have someone show him half the devotion and loyalty Lark gave Amora. Love, that's what he craved. Tasha was the only one he wanted, and he'd fucked things up. How he was going to fix it was the problem.

Stiffening as he caught Tasha's scent and the sound of music. Picking up his mug, he stood, and Ripper made the short walk from the loft to the club downstairs. As he descended the last step, he spotted Tasha at the jukebox. "Isn't today your day off?"

She turned to him with a wry smile and sighed. "I couldn't sleep."

"You okay?" He rested his shoulder to one of the support pillars near her but kept some distance between them. Ripper sensed her relief, and it hurt.

"Too much thinking. Why don't you sleep during the day like Amora? I thought vampires hibernated while the sun was up."

"I'm a hybrid, demon, and vamp. I didn't inherit Amora's sensitivity to the sun. Although, I did inherit her thirst." He raised his mug as she scrunched her nose. Ripper regretted highlighting their differences.

"How did the whole hybrid thing happen?"

The question surprised him. Tasha never asked him about what he was. "Birds and Bees story?" He chuckled as she flipped him off.

"My sweet mother…" Laughing louder as Tasha arched a perfectly shaped brow at him. "Seduced the son of her oldest enemy, well, not so much seduced. They bred out of mutual disdain for Angelus, and I'm the product."

"You never told me the demon thing before."

She slid her hands into her back pockets, and it thrust her plump breasts forward. Ripper couldn't help his body's uncomfortable reaction to the sight. He'd seen Tasha in nothing but a G-string and pasties, okay, not the thoughts he needed going through his head right then. Ripper could picture her perfectly. Her belly dance routine came to mind. Think about unsexy things, Ghoul feeding frenzies, leprous demons, or his demon. That put a halt to naked images of Tasha.

"My demon isn't very pretty."

"And what does it look like?"

"A snake, rattle and all."

"Really?" The surprise was the only emotion that tinged her voice.

"Yeah."

"I always liked snakes."

Ripper dropped his chin to his chest to hide his grin, but not before he noticed her cheeks turned pink. For a woman who performed in barely any clothes or none at all, she was shy. Ripper loved that about her.

"I have to find my own place soon, that part of me likes to hunt and spend time in the water."

"If you're looking, there's a small estate in a parish outside NOLA. The signs have been up forever. It's on the edge of the bayou. Maybe it would work for you."

"Thanks, I'll have to look into it."

He set his mug aside as *Nina Simone's Do I Move You?* started playing.

"Dance with me."

Ripper didn't wait for an answer he took her hands and twirled her into his arms. She fit perfectly against him. She draped her arms over his shoulders as they moved. Their bodies sensuously rubbed, and he felt her heartbeat speed up, and her breath stuttered warmly over his chest through his t-shirt.

"Ripper, I should—"

He dropped his forehead to hers to stop whatever she was going to say.

"Don't say it, just one dance, and I'll let you go. Give me that, please."

Ripper wasn't above begging for this one thing. They'd hugged, hell, even cuddled after hours with the rest of the Revenge crew, but never like this. He craved this connection and Ripper hadn't realized it before.

She nodded as her curves melted into his angles. Tasha's soft moan was loud as he stroked his palms up her back to flatten her large, rounded breasts to his chest. Her tightly furled nipples felt like a fiery brand to his upper abs.

"Ripper."

She whimpered his name as the tip of her nose nuzzled his jaw, over his chin and then the corner of his mouth. Their lips brushed in a teasing game, but she retreated as he moved in. Their breathing mingled during the almost kiss.

"Gods, what you do to me."

"So beautiful." His hands moved down her back over the soft, thin shirt. "Soft and sweet, almonds and cherry."

"Oh." She licked her lips and accidentally stroked his with the tip of her tongue. He felt the prickle of the shift under his skin, and she gasped. "I have to go."

"Tasha, don't, I'm…" Releasing her killed him, but knowing she'd run because she'd seen a hint of his true-self broke him more than anything else had before. This was the second time she'd left him behind. He dropped his head back and scrubbed his hands over his face.

"Smooth one, Jackyl, real smooth," Ripper spoke to the ceiling and avoided checking the door. He could easily pull an Amora and take the next job and the most dangerous bounty he could find. Maybe Ripper was more like his mother than he thought because violence and bloodshed seemed a next viable option. First, he had to find Nicolette for his mother. That would be his sole focus and avoiding his mate should be easy, right?

CHAPTER 4

*T*asha splashed cold water onto her overheated cheeks and looked at the flushed, horny woman in the mirror. She shuddered, and her nipples ached. The impression of every inch of Ripper branded to her. The lean, flat pecs, the defined ridges of his abs, oh gods, the thick, hard cock pushing into her lower belly. For his height and build, the man was carrying a concealed weapon.

Her cunt clenched just imagining the stretch of his thick dick as she rode him. Tasha quickly stripped, then with shaking hands she turned the taps on the shower. Tasha's heart was beating a rapid rhythm as she opened the bathroom closet and pulled down one of her toy boxes from the top shelf.

She released a shaky breath as she removed the top, setting it aside as she removed her favorite shower toy. The thick suction cup dildo felt just Ripper's size. Tasha shifted her slick thighs, pathetic, that's what she was, but she couldn't control the need racing through her veins.

If a dance, teasing, and the non-existent kiss did this to her what would happen if she gave in to just one night with Ripper? Forget her insecurities and doubts, no, she couldn't just have one night. She sighed as she stepped beneath the warm spray. Positioning her toy on the back wall of the stall then she moved under the powerful pulses of water. Her hands stroked the curve of her stomach to her breasts palming the full mounds. She roughly pinched her nipples between her fingers. Fantasy took over, one she'd had with her boss' son as the star longer than she wanted to admit.

It was always the same. He dominated her. Her secret fantasy, but only him in the leading role.

Long fingers with a light sprinkling of hair on the backs splayed on leanly muscled thighs. Her eyes moved over those hands, then up to his pale, green eyes. A thrill ran through her at the look she saw there. His hands lifted then come down on his thighs, a perfect brow rose, and then he repeated the patting of his hands. Bottom lip bit, sucked into her mouth as her stomach clenched. She knew what was coming, knew what he wanted.

Tasha bent at the waist, her fingers hooked in the hem of her skirt and she slowly skimmed it up her rounded thighs. A shiver worked through her as nails score over sensitive, silky skin.

"Lay down." His words and tone offered no option of disobeying. A deep breath, a hard swallow and she bent, lying across his thighs. The heat of him branded her skin through the fragile silk of her dress. He said not one word as he removed her panties over the voluptuous curves of her ass.

A slightly calloused palm smoothed over her flesh. No warning came before his hand connected with her right cheek and goosebumps prickled her skin. Tasha parted her lips to ask how many spankings would be her punishment, another smack and she fell silent. With each spanking, her heart kicked up, pain met exquisite pleasure, and her thighs move together restlessly.

The skin of her ass turned sore and fevered. As she lifted her hips, begging for more, Ripper stopped, making her wait upon his lap.

"Do you deserve another? I believe you are enjoying your punishment too much." She shook her head in denial, and he quickly rewarded her with another sharp slap of his palm. Her head fell forward, and Tasha's eyes closed tightly.

"You were about to lie to me, love. That really won't do. Stand." She didn't question, merely obeyed and rose on weak legs. Tasha's eyes were cast downward, she took in his hands slowly easing his belt free, slipping the button free and then watching the teeth of his zipper separated.

"*Remove your panties.*" She started to speak. "*I did not ask, remove them and straddle me.*" The broad, flared head of his thick cock glistened. Her panties slipped down her legs, stepping one foot then the other out, but left on her heels. He took his cock in hand. Tasha took the two steps that separated them and straddled his thighs.

"*Such a good girl, always so sweet, now show me just how naughty you can get.*" Tasha's teeth sank into her bottom lip as she came forward and she tried to kiss him. Firm lips disappeared when he turned his head.

"*Naughty girls don't get kisses.*"

Tasha moaned, her hands moved to his broad shoulders, and she lowered onto his lap. The broad tip pushed against her soaking wet pussy, stretching her as she clenched tightly around Ripper and she threw her head back. Fully seated, discomfort made her bite her lip as his cock spread her completely. Her hard, throbbing nipples pushed against lace, there were too many clothes in the way, and Tasha desperately wanted skin-to-skin. The fabric of his slacks grazed her inner thighs.

"*Move. Now.*" She didn't even attempt to protest she just began a slow sensuous dance.

Ripper's hand cupped the curves of her ass as she lifted and fell in a steady, unhurried rhythm. Ripper pushed for no more, not yet. His demands were waiting for his control to snap. Her head turned, and his lips were barely a breath from hers. Not touching, but their quickly accelerated breaths mingled.

Her arms twined around his neck, fingers laced as she savored the slow glide. Sinking upon him with a leisurely twist of her hips and lift with an equally deliberate roll. Whimpering as her slumberous eyes opened to meet his in desperation, she silently begged. Ripper shook his head, his lips brushed hers, and he denied her the command for the quicker pace she needed.

Time seemed to stand still, suspending her in a pleasure that wouldn't end. Her speed increased, and he warned her with another palm connecting to her ravaged skin. Flinching, she whimpered with the ecstasy/pain. He pulsed inside her with an almost unperceivable jerk of his cock.

"*Pleas...*" He punished her again.

Repeating the lift and fall as her thighs trembled, lean, strong hands contract on her ass. Ripper's control was on the edge of breaking, and she felt *it in the quickening of his heart. Ripper leaned in, his lips brushed her ear, and his teeth nipped at the lobe.*

"Fuck me." Those were the only words she needed as she began to bounce on his cock, his hips flexed meeting each downward thrust of her body.

Her heart pounded in a breath-stealing pace. Her breasts swayed in the confines of pure white lace. Tasha moved back and forth in hard arches. His tight curls teased over her aching clit each time their bodies connected.

Tasha's head fell back, and upswept curls fell from their confines to fall around her shoulders and down her back. Whimpering moans passed her parted lips as ecstasy swept over her. Her pussy clenched, her thighs tightened, and she wrapped herself around him as the world fell apart.

Tasha came to her senses as her nails painfully pricked her thighs as her legs shook and she impaled herself fully on her toy. Her eyes rolled upward, her stomach contracted, and the rush of her release joined the warm water pounding on her back. The tiles were cold on her ass as she rolled her hips, lengthening her orgasm until she pulled away and the pressure eased as the dildo no longer filled her.

Stepping beneath the water on trembling legs, she washed with unsteady hands before turning off the water and grabbing her towel. Even after her release, a need still pulsed and she knew taking her pleasure into her hands would only ease the ache not take it away entirely. She just couldn't let herself go. Ripper wanted her, of that she was sure, yet she wanted more than a quick fuck. Right now, she wanted a drink, so maybe it was time to hit one of those human bars. If she could find a distraction, maybe just for a few hours, she could forget about the impossibly handsome man she wouldn't allow herself to have.

* * *

THE SILK of her dress seductively moved against her sensitive skin as she stepped through the crush of bodies in the bar. Tasha radiated more confidence than she felt. She performed on a stage each night, hid the few insecurities she possessed and tonight was no different—she put on a show. Her eyes cast around the room looking for the distraction Tasha had come to find. She found a seat at the end of the bar, lifted onto the barstool, and smiled at the gorgeous bartender who came her way.

"What can I get ya?" The woman leaned in so Tasha could hear her over the music and crowd.

"Whiskey on the rocks, top shelf." With a nod, the bartender turned and grabbed a bottle off the top shelf, scooped some ice into the glass and then poured the single.

Tasha picked up the glass, turned on the stool and sipped the potent liquor. Each time a man tried to meet her eyes she turned away. Tasha frowned at the action; this was the reason she came out to the bars. Just one distraction for the night, a body which meant nothing more than a diversion. One-night stands were something she had done many times when she was younger, and sex wasn't something Tasha was ashamed of, but right now she didn't want a nameless hookup.

Disappointment caused her eyes to burn. She had to admit she'd looked, she hadn't been a nun and had even anonymously hooked up. Those nights she had closed her eyes, and instead of the man she was with, she saw Ripper. His beautiful green eyes looked at her with a nearly loving emotion. She dropped her chin and set her rocks glass on the bar, and fingers came up to cover her mouth as she turned away to hide the tears.

She remembered the woman she was, the self-assured one who'd held her chin high and that wasn't who she was now. Had she fallen so low, lost so much of the confidence she possessed? Tasha could pinpoint the moment it had fled. It was the day she realized she was in love with a man she couldn't even wish to possess.

Ripper showed his interest, and he claimed to want her, why couldn't she make her stubborn pride go away? Hell, her body still sang with the pleasure of her favorite Ripper fantasy. Why not take the chance: A broken heart wasn't fatal, or at least she hoped not.

Tasha finished her drink, turned slightly and sat it on the bar beside her. She slid off the barstool, hugged her clutch to her chest and strode towards the door. Once outside, she turned left and walked carefully on her stilettos down the block. No one would hear of this night. Tasha was even a failure at a hookup in a human bar. So much for walking on the dark side and trying to find herself a human for the night. Amora would laugh her ass off at this one. Great, Tasha sighed and continued to walk, less than twenty-four hours from now her humiliation would be complete.

CHAPTER 5

*C*rossing his arms over his chest, the old leather of his jacket pulled tight as stale cigar smoke and the stench of rancid beer settled in trash cans made him snarl his nose. The oppressive heat of the little hellhole of a bar just over the border in a no-name town in Mexico wasn't where he figured he'd spend his weekend. It was a hideout for demons arriving topside. He hadn't told his mother about the mission and he sure as fuck wasn't planning on telling her he came alone.

Lovely women wove through tables in peasant blouses and flowing, thin skirts. Seamus or Fernando—the Alpha and Beta of the pack who'd adopted Amora and himself—could've helped, but he wanted to keep as much from his family and the pack as possible until he had no other choice.

Lark had studied the text in the old tome Dominic—the Order of Angelus' Seer—had too quickly handed over. The mention of the slave trade, preternatural creatures sold as trophies or sexual toys filled the pages. A faded section alluded to the possibility Nicolette made it onto the auction block. Centuries passed since he needed someone with a damn long memory. Going back to Dominic was plan C.

The old demon made his skin crawl, and the less Amora and he owed Dominic, the better.

"Kali." A deeply accented voice spoke his grandfather's name made him bare his fangs. "Easy, you're the one who called me out." He ducked out into the night. The heat wasn't much better out there, but he didn't have to inhale the putrid air inside.

"It's Jackyl. I need to know about the slave trade."

"What is there to say? We're sometimes considered very prized pets." He lifted a brow as the accent disappeared. "Females and androgynous males are highly sought after. You in the market, Jackyl?"

"I'm looking for one of those items, in particular, Nicolette Medina-Jackyl. Dark brown hair and blue eyes. A female vampire not yet reached maturity, Pure-born." He didn't have much information on her appearance.

Kyros whistled through his teeth. "Family?"

"An aunt. This would've happened centuries ago, but I'm sure not many Pure-born have made it to the block."

"This job won't be cheap, Jackyl. People pay high dollar for their pets and civilians aren't privy to the show. I possibly remember a group of young vamp children taken. Don't know if I can find heritage, but they would tally Pure-Born only for special auctions."

Ripper removed his jacket and threw it over the back of a wooden slat chair. The legs wobbled a bit as he lowered his weight to it. Kyros followed and took the seat directly next to his and leaned his forearms on the table.

"Price isn't an option, I want to know everything and don't fuck around. The fee goes down the longer you drag your heels."

"How much are we talking?"

He named a price, and the male whistled again, a greedy light twinkled in his eyes.

"But as I said, the longer it takes for me to get the info I need, I knock off a thousand per day."

"Don't be too hasty, my friend, what you seek isn't easy to come by."

"You have a week, and if I even sniff out a set-up, I'll kill you slowly and without mercy. If you know who and what I am, then you know I'm capable of it."

"The next Collector, the great prophesized one, everyone knows who you are, Medina-Jackyl. Your existence even gives the most high-level demons nightmares. Management would try to kill you with the least provocation, but demons like to keep their heads. They sure as fuck don't want to take on Amora, Demonus and you."

"Remember it. You have my contact info. You have a week. Then I start knocking off zeroes on your fee. Understood?" Kyros merely nodded. Ripper reached behind him and grabbed his jacket as he closed his eyes and felt the shift, the prickle of dematerialization as he focused on his next stop. He appeared silently and walked into the little shop with the blacked-out windows.

Selena Morrivan sat behind the counter at her usual post. He'd known the woman for two centuries since his mother briefly took the then young witch as a lover. The erratic nature of the relationship hadn't changed, sarcasm between the two a beautiful form of verbal art.

After the two women had parted, he had remained in contact with Selena. She looked up from the book she was reading and clear, bright eyes belied the age of the woman he'd come to see.

"Ripper, my boy, what do I owe for this surprise?"

He smiled at the wizen old lady behind the counter. She pushed up from a stool, and he rushed forward to grab her arm. Selena patted his cheek with a gnarled hand.

"Always such a gentleman, even when you were a boy, can't say we can thank that mother of yours."

"Don't start, Selena, you didn't like being in my mom's bed any more than she liked you there when the afterglow faded."

The old woman cackled and patted his arm. "Please, that is one of few lovers I'd sell my soul to forget if I hadn't already that is."

Ripper chuckled and leaned down to kiss the paper-thin skin on her cheek.

"Wow, sell it twice, if I correctly remember, I still have nightmares from the nights the two of you tangled in the room next to mine." He wasn't joking about the nightmares. Rough sex sounds and then the violence of an argument lulled him into a hellish dream every night Selena and Amora were together. How the two had survived their on again off again fuck-and-go amazed him.

"I didn't say it wasn't fun, young man. How is that Amora?"

"Like you don't know she's mated to Lark, committed and all, even got the patter of tiny adopted feet around the house." The gasping wheeze as she clutched her chest and leaned into him as she feigned shock made him snicker. "Knock it off," Ripper laughingly ordered.

"Don't shock a heart like that, I have at least another century before my marker is called in, I want to enjoy it."

He helped her take a seat in a padded chair in the back as she studied him with too wise eyes.

"What brings you to see me? I won't complain, I missed you, but I ain't mistaking that look for anything but a mind running from trouble."

"Read for me?" he asked for the hundredth time, and he always knew the answer he would receive.

"I won't do that to you, Ripper, there is no peace in knowing the future especially one as long as yours will be. Reading for you or Amora will never happen."

Ripper took the seat across from her, leaned forward and rested his elbows on his knees. "I met my mate." He looked up to watch her through his lashes.

"Old news, even this reclusive witch heard."

"How?"

"Haven't you learned that when it comes to a Jackyl nothing much stays hidden. Preternatural creatures are a gossiping lot."

"Yeah, between the killing, feeding, and escaping hunters the bull-shit gets deep."

"So tell me about your mate. A lovely young woman I bet."

"She doesn't want anything to do with me, with what I am."

"Do you know that for sure? You are an exceptionally handsome specimen, and if I even remotely thought I was up to the task, I'd change just for a go."

He arched a brow, and she instantly cackled. Selena's imprisonment curse kept her isolated, and she took her amusements where she could. In that respect, she reminded him of Dominic. It was one of the small reasons he slightly pitied the demon.

"I couldn't even remain straight-faced for that one, but I was telling the truth about you being a prime catch. What did you do to her?"

"Selena! Why must I have always done something?"

Selena gave a disbelieving snort, and he leaned back letting out a heavy sigh.

"My demon partially showed himself the other night, and she ran from me."

"Is that what made her run?"

"What else? As you said, I'm exceptionally handsome." Ripper winked to the old witch's great amusement.

"You are full of shit, too much like your mother. Your ego would topple pyramids with the force of its mass."

"I will not argue with that, my lovely Selena, you are quite familiar with who raised me. How have you been? Drained any unsuspecting men dry lately?"

Selena let out a long-suffering sigh. "Why couldn't I fuck a beautiful woman to maintain my life?"

"It's called punishment, Selena."

"I don't think imprisoning that old demon was worth this, it's not like I didn't let him out. It was for his own good."

"Selena, I don't think the whole concept of no means no had the same meaning as it does nowadays." The loud harrumph made him let out a loud belly laugh, and she promptly swatted him with an old cane within reach of the old woman. "Hey, delicate goods here, Selena."

"Delicate my old witch ass, and don't think I didn't notice you turn the subject away from your mate. How long have you known she was meant for you?"

"The moment I met the raven-haired beauty."

43

"Curvy and gorgeous?"

He nodded, and her thin, wrinkled lips pulled into a small smile.

"Definitely like your mother. How long ago was the moment you met her?"

"Nearly a decade."

"Wow, and have you imprinted on your mate?"

"Not until recently."

A dry snigger made him roll his eyes because he knew what was coming.

"I bet her hormones are in overdrive when you're around. You are not a nice man, Ripper."

"She's much stronger than even my powers, Oh Wise One." Her stubbornness was a crushing blow to his ego. It was easier to joke about it than let everyone know how much it hurt—even though most of them assumed it devastated him.

"Make us a cup of tea, and you can tell me more of your lady. I'm nowhere near ready for our visit to be done."

Ripper pushed up and headed for the small apartment at the back of the occult store. Starting the kettle, he went through the motions of preparing tea as his mind slipped back to Tasha. Ripper had kept his distance from her since Monday.

The distance he remained from his mate killed him. If he wanted advice on how to truly woo his mate, as Lark suggested, Selena might be able to help. Selena had always been his first stop for help when he needed serious answers and not ones dipped in sarcasm from his mother.

"What's going on in that head of yours?" Selena's voice came from behind him.

"How do I woo my mate?"

"What have you done in the past?"

Ripper grimaced as he remembered how he talked partners into bed. It was usually a nameless fuck and her walking out the door the next morning or right after the orgasm. "Does going up to a woman in a bar and asking her to fuck count?"

"You are one smooth bastard, Jackyl."

Ripper pivoted and handed Selena a cup of tea on a pretty matching saucer.

"I haven't exactly grown up with a romantic role model. Before Amora got her mate's attention by attacking her during a bloodlust, she smelled lust on a female and pounced."

Selena sipped her tea. "Perfect, at least you remembered something I taught you. Back to the subject, it's correct your mother isn't romantic. I can't blame you for your disgusting behavior. Have you asked her on a date?"

"You mean like dinner and a movie?"

"No, like monkey sex in a flea-infested room with the post-coital picking of said fleas off each other's naked bodies. Yes, dinner in a nice place with real napkins. The conversation doesn't involve talk about cock or pussy, or the entering of one into the other. Also, a movie that's not softcore porn used as some weird form of mortal foreplay."

"Wow, this is tough, real napkins?"

"You're an asshole, get out." Selena pointed her cane toward the door.

"I'm joking, so you think someone I've had a friendship with would want to do all those dating things with me?"

"Your mate will love those things. It will also show her you're not pulling the same old Ripper bullshit and she's not one in a long line. Because you may not think so, but your reputation does precede you."

"Okay, nice non-sexual date. Conversation. No fucking on the first date. You're not making this very appealing."

"Too damn bad, women like all that shit and you're going to do it because she's important to you."

"Okay, I'll make notes, maybe you can write some conversation points on index cards for me."

"Drink your tea. I'm done talking with you."

"Don't be so cranky. Sit down and rest your fragile old bones."

"Kiss my fragile ass."

"I love you, Selena." Ripper leaned down and kissed her cheek. "Thanks."

"Anytime, Ripper. Out of the handful of good things between Amora and me, you're the only one that I missed."

"I missed you too."

"Don't be such a stranger. It's not like you have an issue with traveling."

Ripper nodded and began to make plans for a date with Tasha. A real date. It would be his first one, and he crossed his fingers that he wouldn't fuck it up. As much as he was already fucking up with his mate. There wasn't much he got wrong in life, yet it figured the most important thing—Tasha—he'd be completely useless. He sipped tea and gossiped with Selena for a while longer before heading home.

CHAPTER 6

The mouthwatering scent of strong coffee pulled her deeper into the shop, and she took a place in line. A little boy ran by and knocked into her legs. She smiled as a harried mother apologized and continued to pursue the bundle of energy. Tasha pulled her phone from the front pocket of her backpack and checked the time. Her days seemed to go so slowly when she wasn't working. Today was her usual day off, and all she had to do was go pick up Meadow for ballet in an hour.

She took a step forward when the line moved. The fine hairs on the back of her neck lifted and Tasha turned to scan the room. No one seemed to be paying attention to her. She shrugged her shoulders, turned forward and texted Lark she'd be there to get Meadow soon.

Part of her wanted to ask if Ripper was home. Not because she wanted to see him, but more to avoid him. One side of her wanted to be near him, and the other wanted to run away.

She hadn't seen him in a week, and he hadn't even come to watch her perform. She hadn't realized how much it would hurt that he didn't show up. Ripper never missed one of her performances when he was in town. She hadn't realized how much she loved when he came to Revenge. No matter where he was in a room, she instantly sensed his presence. Since the day Amora hired her, and the vampire waved him over, Tasha was drawn to him.

Insecurity and desire warred, and Tasha relegated Ripper to being only the boss' son. Two years had passed before she'd discovered who the people she worked with were.

As she aged, Ripper stayed beautiful, and he may hate it, but he was gorgeous. Except for his penchant for an annoying habit of outrageousness, he didn't seem to have many bad habits. Tasha didn't blame him for a lot of his bad habits since most of them he shared with Amora. Tasha found herself smiling and silently chided herself.

Her brow furrowed as she turned again. The feeling of being watched increased the longer Tasha stood there. Her fingers rubbed the back of her neck as she slipped her phone back into her bag.

Tasha stepped up to the counter quickly ordering her coffee. A cold chill ran over her at a considerable pressure at her back, and she turned, knocking her hip painfully against the counter. An older gentleman in a suit that had to cost a small fortune stood a few feet from her—his stare cold as he scowled at her.

"I should have known my grandson would pick the most inappropriate mate."

He shook his head in disgust as his gaze traveled over her, and she shivered. Tasha took a step back trying to put more distance between them, but he moved no closer.

"Do I know you?"

"Angelus Kali, Ripper's grandfather, I was informed he'd claimed his mate. My information must have been false. You are a plain looking human."

"Thanks, nice to meet you too."

"Your sarcasm makes you even less attractive. That bitch of a mother he has is a rather substandard influence."

"Not that it's any of your business, Mr. Kali, but Ripper is not my mate, and I doubt Amora would tolerate your name calling."

A blond Adonis stepped to Kali's side. They bore the same striking handsome looks, where one was dark the other light. She gasped at the green eyes that exactly matched Ripper's.

"Father, I think it's time for you to walk away. This young lady doesn't need to be harassed by you, and I'm quite certain Ripper wouldn't tolerate your attitude toward his intended."

"I'm not Ripper's intended, you're both—" A dark blond brow arched, and Ripper instantly came to mind, her face flamed.

"That is yet to be seen. I believe your coffee is ready, and I'll walk you to Amora's so you're not late for your appointment."

The blond shot the older man, well, not a man, a look, and Kali clenched his jaw as he turned. She rubbed her eyes as he seemed to disappear into thin air.

"Yes, dear, he's not subtle."

"You're Ripper's—" She turned, paid and quickly grabbed her coffee. Breaking out of the line, Tasha spun to find the stranger watching her with kind eyes. "Fuck, you're beautiful, now I know where Ripper—"

"Thank you, you don't have much of a filter, do you?"

Tasha grimaced and tried not to die of humiliation. "Normally it's better than telling a stranger he's beautiful."

"I'm Demonus. I helped create Ripper. I suspect I won't be as pretty in twenty minutes after Amora finds out I've returned from the primordial ooze or the fiery depths of Hell without warning. My best friend doesn't care for surprises." He took her hand and tucked her arm through his. "My son chose well."

"I'm not—" He patted her hand, and she stopped talking.

"Any creature in your vicinity thinks you belong to Ripper. My son has claimed you, not fully, but his scent is all over you."

"Would Ripper claiming me as you said account for a particular female not being hit on in over a year?" The mellow laugh vibrated in Demonus' chest.

"My son never really learned to share. As an only child and being Amora's son, it's understandable."

"Bastard!" The tall man's laughter increased in volume, and she was close to being offended.

"It's not funny; a human woman has needs, and your son is a cock-blocker!" She elbowed the man as he stopped walking and bent over

49

in laughter. "Stop! I almost have sympathy for Ripper with Amora as a mother and now you. I've been in your company less than ten minutes, and you're already annoying." Tasha huffed and walked off leaving the infuriating man to follow.

"Tasha, my dear, I'm sorry."

She might have been inclined to believe him if his voice wasn't filled with amusement at her expense.

"I'm sorry, it was rude of me." Demonus placed his hands on his chest and bowed slightly.

"Does that normally get you out of trouble?"

"Mostly."

"Well, you're shit out of luck this time, and when I see your son, I'm kicking his ass."

With angry steps she headed down the block, Demonus easily keeping up with her. How dare Ripper pull that claiming stuff? It was unfair. She ripped her keys from the front pocket of her bag and unlocked the door.

Tasha stepped inside and left the door open behind her to allow Demonus to follow her. She inhaled the cool, liquor-laced air of the club and the familiarity eased her tensed muscles a bit.

"Sonofabitch, Amora!"

Tasha spun on her toes as Amora sent another fist into Demonus' nose and a smile bloomed on her face at the man's obvious pain. She hadn't even seen her boss' approach.

"I'm glad to see your sweet disposition hasn't changed." His words muffled behind his hand as he held his nose.

"Fuck you, Demonus. You're supposed to be dead or what-the-fuck-ever. I'm sorry to see the rumor floating around the last three months wasn't true. I may remedy that. What the fuck are you doing here?"

"Angelus left the compound and made a trip here, I found out, and I followed. He doesn't approve of our future daughter-in-law."

Her jaw dropped as Amora darted a look at her and grimaced.

"You didn't open your mouth, did you? Ripper will be pissed."

"Um, am I the only one that doesn't know?"

"Not anymore, Tasha." Lark slipped an arm around her waist and gave her a sweet smile.

"You too?" Was she lost in some parallel universe? Or possibly still in her nice warm bed dreaming? Because this had to be a nightmare because her life couldn't have veered this far into some surreal hallucination. She was some demon's mate—whatever the hell that meant —and everyone knew, but her. Was she that blind?

"Ripper isn't known for his tact, you've known him far longer than I. This shouldn't come as a surprise, Tasha."

Lark comfortingly patted her back before stepping away and toward Demonus and Amora with a sweet smile.

"You must be Demonus. I would lie and say I've heard so much about you, but I won't. Do demons need ice or will you be fine? You're not a crier, are you?"

The sarcasm in the woman's voice was thick, and she'd never heard quite that tone from Lark before. The woman was the sweetest creature she'd ever met. Maybe Lark was more like Amora than Tasha believed at first. Nothing could surprise Tasha anymore. It was turning into a weird day.

"Yours?" Demonus shot Amora a look, and the vamp smiled proudly.

"Very much so."

She rolled her eyes and walked away as she went in search of Meadow, leaving the crazy people to their conversation.

A tension headache intensified with every minute that passed, and if it weren't so early in the day, she'd start drinking. Her day off was not going the way she planned.

First, Angelus Kali looked at her like she was a disgrace. Second, Demonus nearly pissed himself laughing at her predicament and lastly the knowledge of her belonging to Ripper was common knowledge to everyone but her. Fuck it; she was having a drink.

Tossing her bag on the bar, she ducked beneath the apron and set her to-go cup beside her bag. She grabbed a shot glass filling it with tequila before grabbing a lime and salt shaker. She shook salt on the lime and took her shot. What the hell did it mean to be mated to

Ripper? Did that explain the uncontrollable attraction she had to him?

All today did was give her more questions she would never have the answers to. Another shot went down, and the conversation between Lark kept Amora and Demonus under control by playing referee.

Huge blue eyes peeked over the edge of the bar and Tasha smiled as Meadow climbed onto one of the stools. "Hiya, Kiddo."

"Hi, Tasha, are we gon' dance today?"

"You know what?" She turned and opened the cash register pulling out some quarters. "Let's skip class and dance right here. What do you say?"

"Yay!" The little girl held out her tiny hand, and she placed a dollar's worth of quarters in her palm. With a squeal, Meadow slipped to the ground and took off running. Unease still lingered after the coffee shop, and she wouldn't do anything to put that sweet little girl in danger. Chair legs screeched over the floor as Meadow climbed onto it to reach the buttons. Tasha took the remaining change and joined the little girl to pick out songs to dance to; she set her chin on Meadow's shoulder as the little girl giggled and she felt her world shift to semi-normal. Well, as ordinary as a burlesque performer at a club run by a vamp and frequented by things that go bump in the night could get to it.

CHAPTER 7

ootfalls rang off the walls as he walked through the empty house and the old oak floors creaked under his feet. Six bedrooms were too much, but he loved the estate. The real estate agent, a beautiful, middle-aged woman in a professional suit, hovered nearby. This was a house he could see spending a life with Tasha in. Not that they were anywhere near that kind of move. Ripper still needed to put Selena's plan into motion, and for that, he needed to get Tasha to take him seriously about a date.

He ran his hands over the wood mantle above the stone fireplace. Something in him calmed as soon as he'd walked through the massive front door.

The price had dropped several times due to the history of the land. Superstition was second nature in the south especially in places like NOLA. None of that bothered him. He smiled as he recalled the story of the alleged witch who had owned the property before her death twenty years earlier. Distant relatives had cleaned out and sold everything inside, yet hadn't been able to sell the house or land.

"The house needs a lot of work. Would they be open to a counter offer?"

The price quoted when he'd inquired about it was more than fair, but just because he could afford it didn't mean he couldn't attempt to get it for less. He hadn't amassed the fortune he had by spending more than necessary. Besides, he hated bounty work and preferred only to take the odd job when the reasons were valid.

"I am sure the family would be open to an offer, were you interested in making one?" The wistful tone in her voice was evident.

That hopeful look in her gaze told him everything he needed to know. She'd probably been saddled with the property for years, and now there was a potential buyer.

"Yes, I'd like to discuss it. I think that'll work well for me. I'll arrange for an inspector to come out. After I get their report, then I'll decide on what I will willingly pay for the property."

"Very well." The cheerful notes were gone.

"Could I stay for a bit alone, get a feel for the house and make sure this is exactly what I want."

"Yes, sir, as you can see the property is deserted. The locals in the nearest town don't come out here. We've been lucky in that regard. Vandalism is sometimes a problem in rural areas. Bored teenagers and all. If you'd lock up when you're done, I'll come out later this evening on my way home and do a final check."

Ripper shot her a charming smile as her cheeks turned pink.

"Thank you, Ms. Daniels. I'll be in contact as soon as I arrange for an inspector."

He nodded and turned his back; she spoke a quiet goodbye and left. Ripper waited until he heard her car pull out onto the main road. Locking the house, he strode into the backyard and headed toward the smell of water.

He entered a copse of moss-covered trees, the soil under his feet squishing as his boots sank into the wet earth. The broken, slightly submerged planks of an old dock came into view. With a sigh he took one look around, sensing no one he stripped and hung his clothes on a low-hanging limb.

The warm, humid air stroked his skin, and he closed his eyes. The pain he'd experienced at his first shift was now a mere discomfort. Bones cracked, his gums burned as fangs pushed through. His skin prickled as he opened his eyes to watch the wave of onyx skin streaked with vibrant emerald appear. His lower body elongated, legs became one, and the soothing rattling sound joined the sounds of birds and the whisper of paws in the underbrush.

Serpentine movements of his true form fluidly flowed as he leaped off the shore and into the murky depths of the bayou. His flattened nose sealed to keep out the water and he continued lower, debris, trash, and fallen limbs littered the bottom.

The water caressed his skin, and he lost himself in the freedom he felt. It was a dual-edged sword—a heavy burden—existing between the human appearance and this form he sadly felt more comfortable in the older he became. In his younger days, he'd barely spent any time as his serpent except for the occasional swim or during battle.

Now though, his demon needed increasing freedom—more blood and violence. What terrified him though was the fact he no longer seemed to have control over him. More often than not they co-existed, but those times were coming less frequently.

Which made a life with Tasha seem impossible. Selena had tried to comfort and bestow her wisdom upon him, but it had fallen on deaf ears. The dating sounded like a plan, although he didn't know if it would be enough.

He'd resisted his demon this long, and he could continue to do so. Ripper could handle the physical pain, suffer through the searing torture of his spiteful demon half. What he couldn't live with was the look of disgust in his mate's eyes. He'd barely shifted, just a small push to the surface and she'd run from him. Concealing him would have to work until he could win her trust. He only needed more time.

His body rolled and forcefully pushed toward the surface. He emerged to feel the sudden breeze on his skin before he disappeared once again into the depths below. He pushed himself, trying to forget in the exertion of exercise. Later he would hunt. He just needed time to think about something other than the mate he couldn't claim and his mission to find Nicolette.

Merely a moment of peace and comfort of being what he truly was, yet forced to hide.

* * *

AN HOUR later he walked into Club Revenge feeling a bit lighter after letting his demon out to swim. He opened his mouth the call out to see if anyone was awake and froze at Tasha's enraged voice.

"Ripper Medina-Jackyl, you snake in the grass bastard!"

Ripper started to back out the door he'd only taken a step into when Tasha's pissed off voice made him flinch.

"No one here by that name."

"You take one more step out that door, and you will regret it."

His shoulders drooped, and he stepped deeper inside the club letting the door close behind him. Tasha stood glaring at him with her fists rested on her generous hips.

"Can I just say how sexy you look today?"

She pursed her lips, and he wanted to nibble on the plump curves. Fuck, his mate was one hot female when she was pissed off. Ripper tried to contain the smirk, but it broke through, and she sneered at him.

"Cut the bullshit. What is this mate thing and why am I just hearing about it?"

"Ma," he hollered.

A snicker came from the direction of the bar, he darted a look, and his eyes went wide.

"Demonus, if it isn't the demon sperm donor. Weren't you supposed to be dead the last few months?"

"Hello, Son. It's a long story. Um, we'll talk later, right now you have some feathers to smooth." The amusement was thick in his father's voice as the man nodded toward Tasha.

"I'm waiting."

"This wasn't exactly how I wanted to have this conversation, especially not with an audience." Hoping his family would get the hint was an exercise in futility as they watched them with rapt attention. Amora poured more shots while Demonus grinned and Lark smiled at him with maternal affection.

"Now or never, Ripper, make the choice, or I'm going home."

Ripper dropped his chin. He planted his hands on his slim hips and took a deep breath in then exhaled heavily. He stepped forward and strode toward her. Taking Tasha's arm, he led her to a quiet corner, partially hidden from the trio across the open room.

"Tasha, listen, I—" Why was it so hard to get out? It's not like she didn't know already. His family opened their mouths, but the sight of Demonus, which probably didn't bode well for Ripper, worried him. Tasha seemed homicidal.

"Speechless doesn't work for you. How long?" Ripper exactly knew what she was asking, but how did he tell her?

"I knew the moment I caught your scent across the room. You were wearing your tight secretary outfit, pinstriped skirt, white blouse, for a number you were performing. Fuck, you were gorgeous." The roll of her eyes infuriated him. "Why the fuck is it so hard for you to take a compliment from me?"

"Because you give them so quickly."

"When I am here, have you ever seen me leave with anyone? Tell me one time, and I'll leave you to the safety of your precious bubble."

When he wasn't there with his family, he fulfilled his needs, anonymous women who meant nothing beyond one night. Ripper may be considered a bastard in many ways, but he wouldn't rub Tasha's face in his conquests. The more he saw her search her memory the further her anger receded. "You've treated me like a kid for the last five years, practically patting me on the head. Before that, you treated me like a friend. I've tried to tell you, and you shut me down every time."

"You're just—" She closed her mouth so fast her teeth clicked together.

"What, pretty, I'm getting tired of that one. Just give me a fucking chance, maybe even a date or a conversation where it doesn't end with you running from me." A snicker from the bar narrowed his eyes. "Shut up, Ma!"

"Amora, your son is trying." Lark moaned as the admonishment ended.

"Could I possibly do this without the audience?"

"Maybe I could suggest some poetry, or a kiss, something to make her forget you have the appeal of a leprous rage demon."

"Dad, so not helping here." He shot Tasha a glare as she coughed to cover what suspiciously sounded like a laugh. "Don't even start finding this funny. Can we go somewhere else to talk?"

"Okay."

Ripper reached out and laced his fingers through Tasha's; turning, he led her toward the door flipping off his parental units as he went.

"We love you too, Son." Ripper glared at the amused trio as he pushed open the door and stepped out into the bright afternoon sun as he tugged Tasha to his side.

"You don't have to hold my hand. We're not on a date."

"What if I choose to ignore that fact and consider this one?" He caught the shrug of Tasha's shoulders.

"It's your delusion." He rolled his eyes and hoped for control.

"I don't like you," Ripper growled.

"I don't like you either," Tasha spoke with a crooked smile, and he started to grin.

With an as solemn expression as he could muster, he turned to her to see her pupils dilate showing her interest before she arched a brow. "Wanna fuck?"

"Not in your wildest dreams, Jackyl."

"You are a shitty liar, Tasha, but I'll let it go—for now." Ripper turned his head forward and continued their walk in silence. Tasha's body moved a bit closer to his the farther they walked. He lifted their linked hands to his mouth and brushed a kiss to the backs of her fingers. A bit of hope bloomed, maybe this would work out after all.

CHAPTER 8

They pulled off the road onto a long drive to the house she'd told Ripper about. She didn't know why she agreed to spend time with Ripper. This wasn't keeping her safe from doing something she'd more than likely end up regretting. "What are we doing here?" Tasha asked nervously.

"I'm thinking of buying it."

She shot him a look as he slipped from the front seat and closed the door, her gaze followed him as he walked around the front of the car and opened her door. He offered her his hand, and she took it.

"Moving here? I didn't think you'd do it."

There didn't appear to be any neighbors for miles, and a breeze stirred her hair. Quiet, it was so different from being in her little apartment in the middle of NOLA.

"Wasn't thinking about it actually, I called the agent and set up a meeting today. When we did the walk through it felt right." He flashed her a crooked grin. "As much as my mother drives me completely insane, I miss her while I'm a nomad. Hell, I even miss the munchkin. It's always been just Amora and me, now, we have a family, and my aunt might be alive. Amora fostered a strong sense of family."

The wistful tone of the handsome man's voice surprised her.

Amora had changed a lot since Lark, but she hadn't considered how the addition of others to the family unit affected Ripper.

"You like your new family?"

He stepped away, and she watched him slide his hands into the front pockets of his jeans drawing her gaze to dangerous territory. Clearing her throat, she darted her eyes away as she pretended to take in the scenery.

"It's nice. We've always had an extended family. Seamus' pack and other assorted misfits. What about you? You've never mentioned family before, parents, or siblings?"

"I have them, but Amora and the ladies are more family than my blood relatives ever have been. I have two sisters, feminine perfection and brains as well, my parents are very into appearance. As you can see I'm not—"

All words and thoughts ceased as firm, yet soft lips pressed to hers and her arms twined around Ripper's neck. The kiss was hungry and desperate, no finesse caused by years of pent-up need.

Tasha whimpered as she felt her feet leave the ground and her legs immediately circled Ripper's slim waist. Rough, muffled breaths were loud as she felt herself being pushed back against the car. He pulled back with ragged breaths and roughly removed her t-shirt. The color of his eyes shifted and changed as the pupil narrowed into black slits as he looked at her.

No words exchanged, she swallowed hard and licked her lips as he just let his gaze stroke over her curves. He dropped her shirt to the ground and brought his fingertips to her breasts. A breath shuddered from between her lips as he traced the edge of the plain cotton cups to the front catch.

He growled, and her thighs clenched as his forked tongue flicked out passed his lips. "I have dreamt of this." Ripper flicked open the plastic fastening, and her breasts fell heavy from the confines of the loosened bra. Ripper looked up at her from under the thick fringe of dark blond lashes. He lowered his head so slowly, and her back arched as the slight sting as his tongue struck her stiff peak.

She nearly came as the twin tips pinched her nipple mere seconds before warm lips wrapped around her nipple and sucked. Her fingers sank deep into the raw silk of his hair. All intentions of protesting dissolved as he tortured one nipple then the other.

Her skirt found its way over her hips as she felt the soft cotton of her panties gave as he ripped them from her with a flex of his hands. Nervousness took over, intensified her trembling, as fear of what it would be like for Ripper to fuck her and the scary thrill of being caught.

"We could..." Fangs pricked her skin with a pleasurable prick, and she threw her head back. Ripper straightened pulling off her nipple as the hard suction gave and he reached back over his head and grabbed the back of his shirt.

Perfect tanned skin stretched over lean muscle, and her hands explored the angles and traced the defined planes of his chest. She leaned her head forward, and her lips found the side of his throat, nipping and licking over the tiny mark as she released his waist and slid to the ground.

"Tasha?" The question gruff as she kissed her way down his chest, the center of his abs and her trembling hands worked at his belt.

"I've thought about this many times. If I'm dreaming, I'm taking advantage."

She roughly worked his pants open and pushed the denim over his hips. A thick, hard dick sprang from the confines of the fabric. Lifting her chin, she caught his lips in a quick kiss while her fingers wrapped around the pulsing length. A moment of hesitation took over, and he must have noticed.

"Suck me."

Tasha nibbled her bottom lip, and then she dropped to her knees as he braced his hands on the roof of the car and watched her with a heavy-lidded gaze. Her tongue stroked her lips, and he groaned. Lifting her left hand, she cupped his heavy sac, rolled his balls in her palm as she parted her lips and closed them around the broad, flared head.

Ripper's hips shallowly thrust, and she relaxed letting him slide all the way to the back of her throat. The silky glide of skin along her tongue and the flavor of pre-cum burst on her senses, Tasha's thighs trembled.

"Fuck, love." A husky whisper followed by an agonized groan as she relaxed her throat and took him all the way. His pubic curls teased her nose as she contracted her throat muscles around the tip, retreating as strong fingers tangled in the hair at the back of her head.

Her cunt clenched as he held her head still and fucked her mouth in long, firm strokes and she took each one. She increased the suction as he withdrew just to hear that growling hiss and she watched the slithering of his forked tongue, the beautiful hints of onyx patches of skin as his demon appeared and disappeared. It showed how much control she had, how good she made him feel.

"So, fucking good, sexy sucking my cock."

Tasha purred along his length as he pushed into her throat once more and froze, the width seemed to expand increasing the pressure. Tasha held her breath as he retreated then took a deep breath through her nose. The pain on her scalp brought tears to her eyes as he tugged her to her feet.

Silky, somewhat thinned lips took hers, and a bitter taste filled her mouth. Her heartbeat increased, the clenching of her pussy painful in intensity as she licked around the lethally sharp points of fangs.

"Do you need me?"

She moaned against his lips as she nodded her head. It was like a drug raged through her blood, the more she tasted him, the thicker her arousal became.

"Tell me what you want."

His voice was a powerful reverberation with a strange hint of a hiss. She nearly came as the forked ends of his tongue tickled the roof of her mouth.

"Fuck me." The words were barely spoken before he turned her and pressed her bare breasts against the warmth of the back window. She glanced over her shoulder as Ripper jerked her skirt over her hips and pushed it to the ground. Strong hands squeezed her hips with bruising force and wrenched her back, so she bent at the waist.

"Say it again, Tasha."

"Fuck me!" The desperation in her voice nearly made her blush, but she had no time as with one deep plunge he took her completely. She screamed as her back bowed upward and her stomach contracted.

Ripper's left hand came to rest flat on the subtle curve of her belly as his hips began a punishing rhythm. Ripper pounded into her, his cockhead abusing her g-spot on every in and out motion.

Her pussy contracted impossibly tight around Ripper's dick, and tears began to burn her eyes. "Ripper, too much." There was no warning before he bit her shoulder, another rush of lust coursed hotly and she slammed her hips back. He retracted his fangs and licked the wound she knew was there.

"No, you can take it."

He snapped his hips forward, his skin meeting her with a sweat-increased slapping in the near silence around them.

"Made for me."

The lean body behind her ground and the pleasure/pain made her fingers claw at smooth metal. "What do you need?" His hand moved between her slick thighs, and he smacked her swollen lips. Her thighs quivered and clenched.

"Open them, Tasha."

She relaxed, and she flashed to all the fantasies she'd had, all the times he'd spanked her, controlled her, and made her submit.

Ripper had asked her what she needed, and she perched on the cusp of more ecstasy than she'd found with any other. She craved it, the rush of something she didn't understand through her veins.

"I, I need you to—" Tasha's cunt clamped down on Ripper's cock, and she dropped her head to the edge of the roof as the flat of his hand repeatedly connected with her aching, inflamed clit. "Fuck me, fuck me," she begged urgently.

Before she had the next plea out of her mouth, steely hands gripped her hips, strong fingers dug deep into the curves, and he took her. Gruff grunts mirrored her high-pitched ones as they were forced from her by the brutal pummeling of his cock into her.

The pleasure built higher, to levels she'd never felt before. The intensity held her prisoner as the cradle of his hips connected with her ass. Tasha was helpless at the mercy of Ripper, and as his body covered her, his hands found the full curves of her breasts. He covered and squeezed, tugged at her achingly hard nipples. His breath hot on the side of her neck.

"Fucking tight."

He groaned as he pushed past the resistance of her clenched muscles and the pain she felt was perfect. Ripper dropped his head to her shoulder as he quickly dropped a hand back to her clit and circled the nub, two strokes were all she needed before her body seized and she came.

A keening cry she didn't recognize as her, broke the air, and she swore she heard Ripper whisper words of love before he sealed their body with one last thrust. As he came, the oddness of the heat filling her had her eyes widening. Panic disappeared just as a smaller, but no less intense orgasm hit her, and she clutched at the arm braced between her breasts while Ripper spilled deep inside her.

CHAPTER 9

*A*nxiety emanated from his mate in tangible waves when he dropped her off at her apartment earlier. She hadn't asked him in, just a quick and awkward peck on his cheek before closing the door in his face. Ripper stood at one of the large picture windows in his mother's loft. He stared out over the lights and listened to the music drifting from the opened doors of bars that littered the block.

"You okay, Son?"

He glanced briefly at Demonus before going back to his study of the bodies wandering the street below.

"I think I did something wrong with Tasha." Ripper searched his brain repeatedly since he'd left her, but he couldn't think of what could've happened.

"And what makes you think that?"

Demonus shifted and leaned his shoulder against the opposite side of the window.

"I don't know. I took her earlier to see the house I'm thinking of buying, and one thing led to another."

Demonus chuckled. "Finally claimed your mate." It wasn't a question, and Ripper nodded.

"She wanted me. I tasted it when I bit her. Then afterward she became quiet. I took her home, and she brushed a kiss across my cheek, sending me on my way."

"Did you explain what being your mate meant? Something like that can be overwhelming for a human female."

"Lark took to it."

"From what I learned today, she grew up knowing about us. Not so much the mating urge, but she's had knowledge of what we are."

"Tasha knows what Amora is, what I am and most of the patrons that come into Revenge." He blew out a heavy breath and pushed his fingers through his hair. "I thought after we were together she would understand."

"Nothing is ever that simple, Ripper. Your mother and I didn't understand the ramifications of having you, a hybrid."

Demonus' words sank in, and he felt it like a gut punch.

"Fuck, we didn't—" Tasha was human, and he hadn't even thought about using anything when they'd had sex. "I didn't even think about protection."

"Son, I'm sure your mother has had this conversation with you."

"Don't joke. It's never been something I thought about before."

"Of course not, it's not like we can pick up diseases or get anyone but our mate pregnant."

"That's not what I meant. I've never forgotten to use one before—this is the first time I've ever gone without." Then what Demonus said hit him. "How did I come to be if Amora wasn't your mate?"

"Just because someone is your intended doesn't mean they feel the same. Can't exactly make a lesbian vamp change her love of women if it's not destined, Ripper. I've known that for a very long time."

"So, Amora is your mate?"

"I don't know. Maybe it was just prophesied, or some trick or spell. Although, if I thought I would've had a chance, I'd have stuck around, I couldn't give her what she needed. I wasn't the one intended to soothe her soul. Lark's that person and your mother is truly happy, happier than I've ever known her to be."

"She is that," Ripper agreed.

"Your mate has yet to conceive."

"How do you know that?"

"Can you feel her, Ripper, sense her every emotion. Does she live in your head?"

Ripper turned to Demonus confused and watched his father wait for an answer.

"No."

"Then your mating wasn't complete, like mine with Amora wasn't. She submitted to you sexually, Ripper, but she didn't give herself completely. Tasha is holding something back. Whether it's out of sheer stubbornness or fear, I don't know. I don't think she's entirely sure of your intentions."

Ripper hated to admit Demonus was right. So much time had passed with Tasha fighting him and resisting the attraction. Patience wasn't a virtue they'd granted him. His parents were both impulsive by nature, Amora more so than Demonus. His Dad kept a tighter rein on his urges; Amora acted first and said fuck the consequences. "So, I have to woo her, huh? You're the third person to tell me that."

"And they're right, Son. You'll have to sweep that gorgeous young lady off her feet and make her fall hopelessly in love with you. Not that I think you need to try too hard. My future daughter-in-law is already in love with you, but she's just not going to admit it." Demonus snickered, and Ripper shot him a glare. "Aside from your mother, I've never met a woman quite so obstinate as your Tasha."

"I know, I love that about her. She's stronger than she thinks and you should see her with Meadow, sweet, maternal."

"Son." The warning in Demonus' voice clear.

"I know, there's too much that needs to be done and resolved."

"Ripper, there's too much you still need to explain. Angelus will probably live a very long while yet, but one day his place will become yours. Your Tasha needs to understand what you'll become, see what you truly are. She has to accept what we hide beneath the surface of our human forms."

That was his biggest challenge, a love/hate relationship existed between the vampire and demon sides. Tasha thought the man she saw was what indeed existed, yet it wasn't. Ripper's demon side was the dominant of the two. If his mating to Tasha was to succeed, then she had to accept more than the human body.

"I don't know if I can ask that of her." The thought of saving her from the fate of being mated to him broke his heart.

"You don't have a choice. You feel the pain of holding the demon too tightly reined. He won't be satisfied with being kept in the dark… your vampire side favored above him. The war will begin, and it'll tear you apart. You have to accept as I did before you."

His father hadn't been around a lot to answer the questions he'd always been curious about. Demonus tried to stay ahead of Kali and other enemies. Most he knew from his travels, studying old tomes and Selena. One thing he always wanted to know popped into his head.

"Why aren't you in line? Why is Angelus so determined I'll rule?"

He crossed his arms over his chest and shifted his body to face Demonus, sadness floated across his father's gaze before it disappeared.

"I rejected it, and Angelus disowned me, struck me from the line. If I'd known it would fall upon you, I'd have accepted my fate and saved you the anguish. I couldn't take the chance of turning into Angelus."

"It's the ultimate power, an endless eternity." What creature or person wouldn't want limitless power and life? Ripper didn't want it, but he grew up knowing what would happen. Someone simply offered it would probably jump right on it.

"I know that now, but hatred so consumed me for your grandfather that I couldn't see past the need to escape. Also, I know there are far better ways to be the Soul Collector than what Angelus taught me. Again, I learned that too late."

"Would Angelus take you back?"

"If I submitted, admitted to my betrayal, renounce everything beautiful I've discovered. That isn't what Angelus wants. You're the one meant to reign, Son. It was foretold by sages nearly as old as Angelus. There is no escaping it. What you need to do is decide how you will take your birthright. Will you rule as your grandfather, cruelly and with an iron-fist or find your way and teach the generations to come? Kali is betting on the former rather than the latter."

"You know what, Pops? You're a real downer."

Demonus chuckled, and Ripper turned his attention back to the window.

"Hey, your mother is the fun-enabling-your-rebellion parent, someone has to be the mean one."

Ripper loudly snorted as he nodded. "Yeah, someone had to be the mean one. You going to be in town long?"

"Your mother asked me the same thing, also Lark, but she was a lot more suspicious when she asked. I don't think that little woman likes me very much."

Lark loved everyone, but she did seem to be hostile toward Demonus. He'd never thought he would see the day that his mother allowed a woman to be possessive, but Amora was just as selfish when it came to Lark. To envy his mom's happiness made him feel like a bit of a shit. His mate was close, he'd tasted her, lost himself in her body, and instead of being with her now, she was in her apartment across the city.

The craving, the urge to wrap around her and keep her close warred with his head that told him she needed her space. Loving and being with him wasn't like committing to a mortal. None of those pesky complications of centuries together, the whole scaly snake demon slithering around the house. No, giving herself to him came wrought with issues piled on top of more issues. Could he ask that of her? Was he even able not to?

"You worry too much about what may happen. Your grandfather isn't dead yet. He'd be if your mother had a say, but she doesn't. Just worry about now, what needs to be taken care of in this time and place, not what may happen in some distant future."

Ripper nodded. "I need to find out if Nicolette survived."

"I heard you were sneaking around the portal. You know that's not the place for you. Every demon within miles of that town can sense you, what you are. Combine the fact you're a Jackyl and the next Collector, Ripper, you're just living with a target."

"I know, but where else was I going to go? The one in Ireland hasn't seen nearly half the traffic as Mexico. It seems every demon or soul that wants to make an escape comes to our shitty little continent."

"True, what other place is better to blend into, American is the cesspool of the melting pot." Ripper grinned and rubbed his palm over his jaw listening to the rasp of stubble. Demonus leaned his back against the wall and tipped his head back. "Kyros won't steer you wrong, he loathes Angelus, and that works in your favor."

"How did you know who I went to see?"

"Kyros is one of mine, he's loyal to me, and I keep him topside. He knows he fucks me over, he's back slaving away as some high-level demon's errand boy or worse."

"And what exactly have you been up to in your absence?"

"You'll find out soon enough. I'm on the board of a company specializing in paranormal interests. It's a well-kept secret, but it won't be for long."

"I don't even want to know. I have enough issues. I don't want to deal with Supernatural becoming a corporation. That just sounds frightening."

"You're right, it is. I'm off to my hotel if you need me, you know where to find me."

There was a hug and a kiss on the forehead, he remembered the goodbye from when he was a child. Demonus would visit him, do the father-son things, then before he left, a hug and a kiss.

"I love you, Son."

Ripper nodded and before he could blink the man was gone. Why did he bother talking with his parents? It merely made him more confused. He wasn't any closer to figuring out what to do about his mate or the mission he needed to complete. It was all a mass of fucked up confusion. Leaving Tasha time to think was scarier than confronting her and getting it out of the way, but he knew it was the right thing to do.

Now if he could decide on the best course of action in discovering the whereabouts of his aunt. Kyros still had time, a few more days. In the meantime, he had domestic shit to take care of, a house to get inspected, a woman to make up with and their home to buy. He had wanted to show her the house, see how she reacted and if it was a place she could be happy. If he purchased a home, it wasn't just for him.

Ripper grunted. If she panicked about sex with him, he sure as hell wasn't going to mention the house he wanted to buy for them. Scrubbing his hands roughly over his face, he wondered how the hell he'd come to this point in his life? If this were what an average mortal went through, fuck, he would start feeling sorrier for them.

Sleep pulled at him, so he strode to his room and walked between the screens. Meadow was curled up in the middle of his bed. Little shit, he snorted as he changed into pajama bottoms and a t-shirt. He squeezed onto the edge of the bed.

"Ripper?" Her sleepy voice sounded as she snuggled back against his side.

"Shh, go back to sleep."

"The bad men were chasin' me." He wrapped his arm around her.

"It's just a nightmare, little miss. Do you wanna get in bed with Ma and Lark?" She shook her head, and he pulled the covers up to her chin. "You're safe. I promised you'd never go back."

"Okay." She paused as he saw little tears catch on her lashes. "The mean man said Momma 'Mora and you would save me."

"Yes, we would. Now, you need to get some sleep. It's late." He didn't know how to reassure a little girl after a bad dream, but he tried. Meadow lifted her head, a grave look on her face, very much like the one she wore a lot after they rescued her.

"Don't save me." The tone was far more grown-up than it should have been and carried an icy edge. He started to demand an explanation, but her eyes closed, and she curled against his side. A cold chill ran down his spine, and he wondered if there was something else he needed to start worrying about and sleep was a long time coming.

* * *

Ripper needed to find more friends along the normal spectrum. He shifted on the cold steel of an autopsy table as he watched Ennis start the Y-incision humming a cheery tune to herself. The bespectacled, sweet-looking woman swayed, and a creepy smile tilted a corner of her thin lips. Yeah, he needed new friends.

No one knew her real age. They'd tasked her with assisting lost souls to the next realm. Heaven and Hell didn't exist, Angels and Demons, even Gods and Goddesses, but not one singular being to rule over all. Creatures like Ennis—Gatekeepers—ushered the newly dead. If you'd actually fucked up, you made it to Mael—the closest place to a Hell that existed.

"She enjoys her job." Epoch's voice came from his left, and he turned to find the slight-built male leaning over the table with his chin rested on his hands. The Ghoul looked so ordinary that no one would ever know he was a flesh-eating creature who hung out in cemeteries.

"Hey, Epoch."

"Hi, Ripper. How's the family doing?"

"Amora is doing great, psychotic as ever."

A lascivious grin pulled at the corners of Epoch's mouth. "I would so do—"

"Stop right there." Ripper shuddered and avoided eye contact with the smirking Ghoul. "Why do people think it's okay to tell me they want to fuck my mom?"

"You just have that kinda face? People like to tell you things— secret things."

"I don't like secret things of any kind. Now quit thinking about my mother."

"Okay." Epoch grinned wider.

"Liar." He turned back to stare at Ennis and ignore Epoch.

"This habit of you and Amora's just to stare at me is rather annoying, Rache."

"Don't call me that. I don't know what the fuck she was thinking." He still owed his mother's payback for that.

Ennis chuckled. "Probably how much it would piss you off later in life."

"Probably."

"What do you want, Ripper?" The sound of bones cracking punctuated her question.

"I have to find someone." Asking Ennis about Nico was his easiest way of knowing whether she was alive or not.

"I'm assuming this someone isn't of the living variety." Ennis set her scalpel aside and straightened.

"My mother's sister, Nicolette."

"Why hasn't your mother ever asked me?" Ennis walked around the table and leaned back against it.

"Amora thought she was dead. Seeing the house burn down with her family inside doesn't leave much room for doubt."

"Poor Amora, does she require comforting," Enoch innocently asked.

"No, she doesn't." He listened to Epoch quietly chuckle. "Bastard."

"What do you need?" Ennis pushed away from the table and straightened the buttons of her white coat.

"Just that easy?" Nothing was ever simple, especially when it came to Preternatural creatures. Ulterior motives were second nature—they always wanted something.

"Nothing is ever that easy, Ripper."

"Then what do you want?"

"Um, let's see. What could I possibly want?" Ennis crossed her right arm over her stomach and rested her left elbow on her forearm to tap her chin.

"Cut the shit, Ennis. What is it?"

"Epoch needs a babysitter."

"He's almost a millennia-old; what does he need a babysitter for?" Supervising a cannibal, just the addition he needed for his resume right after watching a homicidal vamp.

"The whole gnawing the sinew off bones thing."

"Everyone has their quirks." Ennis arched a brow. "Fine, when?"

"Now."

"Road trip," Epoch squealed and then jumped up and down. "I have to pack a snack." He ran from the room.

"Seriously?"

"He loves his field trips. Now, what do you want to know?"

"Did you ever lead a Nicolette Jackyl?"

"No, wasn't on my watch."

A bit more hope bloomed in his chest at Nicolette still being alive. "What do you know about the auctions?"

"Humans are savages. They feed on hate and intolerance. And the ones who know about us think we're monsters. It's the reason we keep ourselves a secret. Unfortunately, sometimes our kind isn't any better. Pure-Born Vampires get top dollar since it's difficult to break them. Your mother is proof of that. It took them decades to do it."

"What happens to the ones that sell?"

"Guard dogs, mostly, but a large number of females are sex slaves. Passed around like party favors. I've heard of a few brothels that specialize in preternatural sex slaves. Again, the harder to break them, anything goes. A lot of suicides came my way. It is their only escape."

"You're just a ball of fucking sunshine."

"One of my many charms."

"I'm ready." Epoch bounced up to the side of the table. He clenched a bag in his slender hands and Ripper didn't want to know what was in there. The stench of blood and new decay was bad enough.

"You're not eating that in front of me."

Epoch gave a heavy sigh. "Spoilsport, for someone who drinks blood, you're terribly squeamish."

Ripper turned his attention back to Ennis and away from her ward. "So, as far as you know, my aunt is still alive."

"A maybe is all I can give you. I missed a lot in my last century as a supervisor, but one like your aunt would have caused quite a buzz. Pure-Borns are notoriously hard to kill. Being a Jackyl would make it tougher."

"Thanks, Ennis, when do you want him back?" The slow smile made him suspicious. "I'm not keeping him."

"Fine, a few hours of adventure should knock down his usual enthusiasm. His perkiness is tiring."

The ghoul currently bouncing from side to side on his toes caused him to shake his head. "I can see that, and we still haven't left yet. Come on, Epoch."

"No alcohol or outside snacks, which the drinking frequently leads to, so keep a close eye on him."

"Got it, he gets the drunk munchies." Ripper jumped down from his seat and headed for the door with Epoch close on his heels. "Don't try to skip town, Ennis, I'll find you."

"Your suspicion offends me. Now, play nice, Epoch."

"Yes, ma'am."

A polite, bouncy ghoul…Ripper already wanted to back out of the arrangement. The echo of footsteps was loud in the long corridor leading to the exit.

"Where are we going?"

"Let's see Amora."

"Really, I find her psychoses incredibly sexy, I bet she wouldn't mind watching me eat—"

Ripper blocked out what he knew was coming next and pushed open the door. He could hear Ennis' maniacal laughter even through cement and steel. If he knew Ennis wasn't so attached to the ghoul, he'd be frightened of being permanently stuck with Epoch. He already had enough problems with an unreceptive mate, a possibly not dead aunt to find and a prophecy that viciously rode his heels.

CHAPTER 10

*L*ark's head was bent as she sat behind Amora's desk going over the receipts from last night and Tasha hesitated before she knocked on the doorjamb. The younger woman smiled brightly as her head popped up.

"Tasha, can't you stay away from this place?"

Any other day she would have laughed at the woman's teasing, but when she didn't, the smile fell. "Can we talk?"

"Oh, this sounds serious, come on in."

Tasha stepped into the dim confines of the room and closed the door.

"Even more grim, a closed-door conversation. Okay, tell Mama Lark what's wrong."

"I did something wrong." Lowering herself onto the chair in front of the desk, she tried to calm her nauseous stomach. Nerves wrecked her usual calm, laidback disposition.

"Do you need Amora to help hide the body?"

The severe tone of Lark's voice brought her head up; no humor alighted in the bright blue gaze.

"No, and you offering Amora up to help hide a body so easily is a bit frightening." She wasn't sure if she still wanted to belong to this family. They were a lot more violent than she'd first assumed. What the hell has she gotten herself into?

"Family does what needs done. So what is this bad thing you've supposedly done?"

"Ripper and I, well, we—" Groaning, a huge grin bloomed on Lark's mouth, and she rolled her eyes. "Don't be happy about it!"

"Why not? From what Amora has told me, you've been dancing around my handsome stepson's advances for quite a while."

"He took me out to see the house he wants to buy. We were talk-ing...I told him a little about my family and the next thing I know he's kissing me." She shook herself at the longing sigh that escaped and glared as Lark snickered. "Right out there in the open. Practically bent over beside the car, anyone could have driven up. What was I thinking?"

"I hope you weren't capable of thinking. Amora does that to me quite often. She's exceptionally fond of making love out of doors. Unseemly, but," Lark possibly wasn't the one to talk to about this. Amora and Ripper were far too similar, and the younger woman adored her mate and stepson.

"You are not helping, Lark," Tasha admonished.

"I'm sorry." The apology would have seemed believable if the woman wasn't wickedly grinning.

"We didn't use anything, Lark."

"Oh." That one exclamation turned Lark's expression serious. "Um, I don't know how much help I can be. Did you speak with Ripper about this? He would be better equipped to answer any reproduction questions."

"I can't ask him." Her voice rose several octaves, and Lark arched a brow.

"Maybe Amora could help, she did conceive with Demonus."

"No!" Tasha fervently shook her head as much as she trusted her boss, she didn't feel comfortable talking about sex with Ripper with the man's mother.

"Demonus, perhaps?"

Leaning forward, Tasha rested her elbows on her knees and hid her face in her hands. "How could I let this happen? I'm old enough to know better than this."

"Things happen in the heat of the moment. If I was straight and Amora was a male and affected me as she does, I don't think it would occur to me either. You love Ripper." Denial danced on the edge of her tongue and Lark raised her hand. "Don't try to deny it. No one is blind, except for Ripper possibly. Finding your mate is a momentous occasion. I don't understand why you fight it so adamantly."

How did she explain what she didn't understand? Ripper was handsome, sweet, flirtatious, and attentive. All these emotions writhed and mixed with years of insecurity.

"Ripper is an exceptionally handsome man, sexy, and I don't understand why he wants me. Not that I don't think I am attractive, I wouldn't feel so comfortable on stage if I wasn't confident. This is about Ripper. He could have anyone."

"Tasha, yes, Ripper could have anyone, he probably has in nearly two centuries, but everything he is craves you. Just you, and if he's as much like his mother as I believe, then he'll cherish what you have together.

"I know Amora has taken countless lovers in her life, yet I know as much as my mate, wife, loves to flirt, I don't have to worry about her taking another to her bed. You must get past whatever is in your head, accept that an incredible man does love you."

"He told me. I don't know if he realizes I heard him."

"Then you need to make a decision and also discuss your fears with him. Because I can guarantee Ripper is no less frightened than you are. You have to accept a lot when you take him as a mate and husband."

"Husband?" Tasha croaked and swallowed hard as she peeked at the smiling woman through her fingers.

Lark's sudden burst of giggling wasn't helping at all. She asked herself again what the hell she'd gotten herself into?

"Go home, Tasha. Enjoy your day off and call Ripper. You two need to have a serious conversation, especially before you start showing with demon spawn."

Tasha's eye twitched and then she glared at Lark. Pushing to her feet, she looked across the expanse of Lark's desk. "You are evil, and now I see why Amora loves you."

The sweetest smile spread across Lark's lips. "Thank you."

Huffing and stomping from the office weren't the most mature options, yet she did it. She was exhausted. If she went home and tried to take a nap, maybe she would feel better. Stress weighed heavy on her shoulders. The talk with Lark hadn't helped at all. She was terrified and confused; Ripper was everything she'd thought she'd want in a man, well, except for the hybrid thing.

She'd been employed by Amora for almost ten years—the best job she'd ever had. To her parents' great disappointment, they thought it was a waste of money putting their middle child through college only for her to become a stripper.

Tasha had lived in a corporate world for three years, and she despised every minute of the monotonous regularity of nine-to-five. Her family barely spoke to her outside the expected holiday calls or visits.

Club Revenge was her family, the ladies, Amora, even Ripper, now Lark. They accepted her, loved her. Walking out into the afternoon sun, she lifted her face to the warmth and slid her hands deep into the front pockets of her jeans. Her head was a fucked-up mess of chaotic thoughts. Longing for the simpler days when her hormones weren't a cyclone of confusion.

Knowing what she wanted and obtaining it was two separate problems. As much as it pained her to admit Lark was right, she needed to accept these feelings between Ripper and her. Her stubbornness, on the other hand, possessed a different idea.

If she didn't work it out soon, her sanity was in danger. Instead of heading back to her apartment, she set off in the opposite direction. A walk would clear her head, but as she strolled and let her thoughts wander, they flashed to Ripper. The flare of lust in his eyes as he'd looked at her and his control slipping as he'd fucked her mouth.

She'd done that to him, an odd surge of satisfaction heated her chest. She rolled her tongue over her palette as she remembered the tickle of the forked ends that teased her and the way she licked around the tips of his fangs. The bitter drops of fluid that had dripped from them. Her thighs clenched at the sensory memories of what they'd done to her.

Craving more, in hindsight Tasha had wanted to drag him into her home and take him to her bed. Not merely for a repeat of the incredible encounter, but to curl against him, have his leanly muscled arms hold her.

She wanted it all, dreamt of what it would be like to belong to Ripper. In the beginning, he was her friend, a silent, comforting shoulder, and as her attraction to him intensified, she had fought her desire to be his lover.

Gods, how life changed with dizzying speed, and she felt there was more going on than her budding relationship. Amora was tight-lipped about whatever was going on. Ripper and her whispering together and the appearance of Ripper's father whom she swore was supposed to be dead. That Angelus person and his talk of mates, her unworthy. Was she even ready for this?

The conversation she avoided with Ripper needed to happen because she needed the truth to why dread made her wary. Was the life awaiting her filled with more danger than it was worth?

CHAPTER 11

The oppressive silence caused a shiver of unease to work up his spine, Ripper fought past it and slipped deeper into the darkness of the castle corridors. After Meadow's warning to not save her, he had to have answers. Ennis gave him part of the information he needed for Nicolette, but Meadow was a new concern to add to the growing inventory.

An hour ago, he'd left Epoch to disgustingly ogle Amora. He didn't know if leaving the ghoul at Club Revenge was such a great idea, but he had shit to do and babysitting a ghoul wasn't on his list of favorite things.

Visiting Dominic again wasn't on his to-do list of the century. He opened the creaking door of the library and proceeded to the hidden chamber imprisoning the demon.

Death, a sickening stench clung to everything. Hell had its own smell, and it filled his nose as he swept the tapestry to the side.

"The young demon returns."

Amusement tinged Dominic's greeting as he stepped into the dark room and let the thick fabric fall to conceal the outer room.

"Wasn't my plan, but I need answers."

"The young girl concerns you. A mere child has brought you here to ask for my assistance."

Ripper didn't understand why he trusted the male, but a mutual hatred was forming an unlikely bond. Dominic motioned toward the chair opposite his in front of the fire, and he slowly strode across the room to take the offered seat.

"She had a nightmare and something she said made no sense."

"What was it she said?"

Clothed in the same dark robe as their first meeting Dominic relaxed back in his seat. His hands with their skeletal long clawed fingers rested loosely on the arms of the chair.

"That the bad man told her that Amora and I would rescue her, then she told me not to save her."

"A child is the greatest of Trojan Horses, innocence no one would ever suspect of great evil."

Ripper tried to hide his flinch, yet the slight quirk of Dominic's mouth showed he failed.

"Are you saying that Meadow isn't what she appears?"

"No, your Meadow is exactly what she appears, but she's special. She can see what others cannot, a beneficial asset for The Order. One they would love to see returned to them."

He sensed Dominic wasn't finished, so he waited.

"I would heed her warning, if they recapture her, do not come for her."

Was the old bastard insane? They would come for her, she was family, and they would fight through Hell for one of their own. His jaw clenched and the muscles ticked as he resisted the urge to argue.

"Are you saying Meadow's psychic?"

"In a way, she's more than that, though. Yes, Meadow can see the future, advise on matters not just of this realm, but her unique gift is she's a Foreteller of Death."

"She's just a baby!"

"Calm yourself, Collector, this child will be of great use to you. Your grandfather has already seen this. She was to become my apprentice, but I advised them her training as a Hunter should come first."

Confusion ate at him. The hits kept coming, and he couldn't keep up. He only thought he would find Nicolette for his mother. Now he was mired in some Preternatural Conspiracy Theorist wet fucking dream.

"Now, why would you suggest that? I'm sure it wasn't out of the kindness of your heart."

"Hardly. I have so few amusements, and Angelus' frustration is a great one." The mirth in the demon's voice made Ripper smile as he turned to stare at the flicker of flames over the logs.

"What is your advice on what to do about Meadow?"

"Protect her, keep her from The Order as long as possible. As you are well aware, Angelus thrives on souls who have no hope, being able to foretell impending death would allow him to amass a great collection.

"A limitless power where he could rule long past the span of his existence. The more he has to feed upon, the stronger he grows, and that doesn't bode well for you when it comes time to destroy him."

"Who says I have plans to kill him?" Emotion nearly crept into his voice, but he quickly killed it as he shot Dominic a look. Bushy white brows rose high enough almost to be hidden beneath the hood of his robe.

"Collector." Amusement brightened Dominic's tone. "We both know you will one day challenge Angelus, and he will push the limits of your family's control. Alas, as powerful as Angelus Kali is, he is not all knowing, tremendous obstacles await him and your family. Ripper Medina-Jackyl is a thorn in a festering wound."

"Is that one of the few amusements you have, Dominic?"

Dominic smirked with a lift of his thin shoulders beneath the billowing fabric and remained silent.

"Against my better judgment, Demon, I like you."

"Go now, Collector. You have much to learn; many surprises await and none will come easily or without much heartache."

Ripper wanted to know more, but he knew in his gut Dominic wouldn't part with any more knowledge tonight. He needed to get back home, and he had a lot he needed to think over and more information necessary before he could bring any of this to Amora's attention. Telling Lark about Meadow was not a conversation he was ready to have.

"Thanks, Dominic." He pushed to his feet, and Dominic remained seated.

"We will see each other again soon, Jackyl. We have much to discuss in the future."

The quirk of the demon's lips caused an unease that hadn't been there during their conversation. Ripper knew the male knew more because there was too much evil mirth dancing in the human-like blue eyes.

Ripper closed his eyes, pictured home and felt the prickle beneath his skin. Weightlessness washed over him before he appeared in the middle of the club. The sun would soon rise, Lark and Amora spent the last few hours together until his mother would slip into sleep for the day. He needed a drink, and then he had to get to work.

* * *

CHERRY BLOSSOMS AND ALMONDS, the scent hit him before he even heard the knock. Ripper lifted his head and smiled as he spotted Tasha. She nervously shifted from the doorway.

"Hey, when do you knock?" Her presence pushed away the heaviness of his troubles. The revelations from his midnight meeting still bothered him, and he was nowhere near having answers. It was why he'd decided to consult Selena.

"You looked a bit busy."

Papers covered the coffee table, and the book they'd received from Dominic laid open on top.

"No, well, I was doing a little research. I have to make a trip out of town tomorrow morning. Come on in, you won't wake Amora, and the others have gone shopping."

The pen he held dropped to the notebook as he stood. She looked beautiful, tight jeans and t-shirt showed off her curves. Her face was makeup-free, and he'd noticed she only wore it when she performed or bartended.

"Ripper, I don't know—" She hesitated and darted her gaze away.

"What's wrong?"

"We, the other day, we didn't use anything and, well, I was wondering how all that stuff worked. Not exactly up on the fertility of hybrids."

Tasha looked everywhere but at him as he walked toward her. Ripper took her hands and pulled her toward the couch.

"I wasn't planning what happened...I didn't even think. We don't suffer human disease, so you're safe there."

His mate chewed nervously on her lip. "That's good, but what about—" She paused.

"Getting pregnant can happen, but you're not."

The quick collapse of her body and heavy sigh nearly caused him offense. What would be so wrong with—Ripper cut the thought off before it formed and gritted his teeth as he calmed his temper.

"That's good, excellent. I've never had to worry about that before."

His thumb stroked over the backs of her hands, fingering the soft skin and felt her tense. The tempo of her breaths increased along with her heartbeat, and a sudden rush of desire filled the air. He lifted her left hand to his mouth to press a kiss to her palm and nipped at the base of her thumb.

"Ripper, that is not why." He brushed his lips against her palm, then sucked slightly at the jump of her pulse. "Gods, that's—" She moaned and bit her pouty bottom lip.

"Why do you fight me, Tasha, you know we're meant for each other." Her eyes closed and her lips slightly parted. Ripper couldn't resist a taste, so he leaned into her. His tongue flicked over the seam of her lips before pushing inside. Lips trembled under his as her arms twined around his neck to pull him flush against her.

A loud growl echoed in the large room at the sensation of her hard nipples through the layers of their clothing. He didn't know how it happened but their bodies shifted on the couch and he came to rest between her spread thighs.

The heat of her pussy was a brand on his lower abs. He took her mouth with teasing thrusts and retreats, and she tasted sweet with hints of coffee and mint. Pressing his hips down, grinding, he made her thighs quiver and then grip tightly to his waist. Her fingers played with his hair and nails scored his scalp. That slight abrasion caused his groans to deepen.

The demon writhed beneath the surface of his skin. Demanding to be let out to claim their mate. His gums tingled as his fangs dropped, the pungent flavor of venom filled his mouth. Tasha let out a keening, muffled cry as her tongue circled the pointed tips gathering the droplets. She increased the arch and roll of her hips as the scent of lust wafted around them.

All doubt left his brain, the poison lethal to all but his intended mate. The acidic fluid capable of burning away layers of flesh with a mere drop. He pushed his hands roughly under her shirt and covered her breasts, palmed the lush curves. Tasha lost herself in his touch, demanding more with sweet arches of her body and desperate little cries muffled by his kiss.

Everything in him screamed *mine* when she was near. She would give herself entirely to him, and he refused to accept any other option. His hands fisted in the cups of her bra, then he flexed his hands and tore the front. Ripper opened his eyes in time to see hers widen. All thought disappeared as he ripped his lips from hers and dropped his mouth to her breast.

He covered the soft olive tone with rough kisses, bites, and sucks. A growl tore from his throat. The forked tip of his tongue was circling the tan of her areola in decreasing rings until he reached the textured hardened peak of her nipple.

"Ripper!"

His fangs pressed into the skin on either side of the peak as he sucked firmly and lashed with fevered snaps of his tongue. Tasha's body jerked beneath him. He loved the sensitivity of her breasts, and he was sure he could make her come just like that. One day he would try, but he needed to taste the intense, tang of desire. Ripper rested on his knees and ripped at the opening of her jeans until the zipper gave and he surged down the couch. He released her nipple with audible sounds that caused her to cry out.

Ripper smirked up at her as she watched him from beneath heavy eyelids. He shoved the fabric to mid-thigh while she shifted her hips and then pushed her legs upward so her knees rested on her chest. The flushed lips of her cunt were rosy with need and his mouth watered. Her hard clit peeked from between; his tongue slithered out and danced teasingly over the nub. Tasha's nails painfully pricked his forearms.

He pushed his elongated tongue into her pussy, hissing at the clench as he tickled over the wet velvet sheath.

"Oh fuck!"

Finding her sweet spot with the tip, he pushed and lapped at it. Her hips moved in a sexy roll taking his tongue deeper. Whimpering and crying out as her nails painfully raked his skin; without seeing he knew red welts scored his arms.

Ripper's tongue glided out to lap at her swollen lips. "So sweet."

A grumble of appreciation issued from his throat as he dived back in. Plunged deep and tongue fucked her as she brought her hands to her breasts, plucked and twisted her nipples until the peaks were rosy with the roughness of her touch.

The sight made his already hardened dick fight the confines of his jeans. Ignoring the intense desire to release his straining flesh, he needed to savor the luscious tang of her cream on his sensitive taste buds.

The realization that he could eat her for hours, days and never get enough was a gut-punch of hunger. She fucked his tongue like a woman possessed. She cried desperate and dirty. The abundant scent of desire was an aura around her. Ripper felt his mate's need running through his veins, the intensity of it beyond anything he'd ever felt before.

She froze as that knot tightened under the insistent ministration of his tongue. Ripper watched with rapt attention as her eyes widened and her mouth fell open in a silent scream. The gush of her orgasm heavily flowed around his tongue. She threw out her arms frantically anchoring herself as she shuddered. He jerked away.

Ripper clawed open the button and zipper of his pants, freed his pulsing cock as he surged to his knees. With one deep thrust, he took her, felt the pleasure ravaged sheath give with a fist like resistance. Her heels tapped on his shoulders as the brutal pounding of his hips connected with loud slapping sounds. Growling as his hands curved over the arm of the couch and his claws pierced the fabric.

The dazed expression of fluttering lashes and eye rolls, the demon took over as his skin changed in a prickling wave. His cock thickened inside her eliciting a piercing shriek as her pussy undulated around the mass stretching her. Control was a wish of the past as he fucked her, driving her into the couch.

His demon howled, coiling tight preparing for the moment he could strike. Somewhere in the distance, he realized nails scored and split the skin of his shoulders and chest. His gaze dropped to where their bodies met, watched as the thick base stretched the dark mauve of her pussy wide. Her body arched upward as he drove her hips down, slamming onto his cock and meeting his thrusts.

An agonized scream broke through the roar of lust flowing hotly through his veins drew his gaze to her face. Her eyes were squeezed shut, tears stained her flushed face, and he lost all thought as he sealed their bodies with one single rough thrust. He filled her with his seed, and his demon struck, his fangs sank deep into her shoulder. She came again with a vice-like clamp milking every shot of his load.

Blood flowed over his tongue as she clutched him firmly in her trembling embrace as his muscles gave and he collapsed on top of her. His fangs released and he licked the twin marks closed as she stroked his sweaty back. Her breathing was ragged as he turned, met her sleepy gaze. A small smile played across her mouth and Ripper couldn't refrain so he kissed her with a tenderness that belied his earlier actions.

"One day we're going to have to do this in bed." His demon retreated with a satisfied hiss.

"I am kinda folded in half here."

He chuckled as he realized the tops of her feet rested on the arm of the couch. Loathing the need to separate their bodies, but he slipped his half-hard flesh from her just as a throat cleared.

Ripper turned his head to find Lark watched with shocked eyes and covering Meadow's with her hand.

"Um, you do have a room, Ripper."

He pulled his jeans up, and with a wince, tucked himself back into his jeans. With quick work, he set a flaming-faced Tasha to rights.

"Sorry, I have to get to work. Um, hi, Lark, bye, Lark." He watched amused as Tasha gave him a quick kiss and ran for it.

"Sorry, Lark."

"You know, apologies work better when you don't smirk." Lark walked to the kitchen shaking her head. "You and your mother need to learn that. Meadow, put your stuff away." Meadow skipped away as if nothing had happened. The beauty of youthful ignorance, he guessed.

"Come on, did you see my sexy mate?"

"All I saw was a tangle of bodies defying logic. You're going to break that poor human girl."

"Thankfully, she's highly flexible."

Small hands shoved at his chest.

"Go shower. I'm never sitting on that couch again." Ripper chuckled, feeling lighter despite his worries. He returned to the offending piece of furniture and grimaced at the mess. "From the look, shower after you clean up. Nasty."

"Like Ma and you ain't made a mess or two."

"We are not talking about that."

Ripper gathered up his papers and books, shoved them in his backpack. Tomorrow was soon enough to take care of the bigger problems. Right now, his issues were easier to resolve.

"You're going to break that poor human woman."

Epoch's voice came out of nowhere, and Ripper turned to find him peeking around the corner of the door that led to Amora's panic room. Epoch batted his long lashes and sweetly smiled.

"What the fuck are you doing here? You're supposed to be

with Ennis."

Amora had dropped Epoch back off with Ennis after his field trip away from the morgue. He didn't need to become best friends with Epoch. The creature had an unnatural obsession with people who paid him attention.

"How the hell did you get away from Ennis?"

Epoch shrugged and looked almost innocent. It was a good thing he knew better.

"You're more fun to observe. Do human females like creatures like us?"

"I don't know about all." Ripper grunted and roughly pushed his fingers through his sweaty hair. "Why am I not kicking your ass right now?"

"I am only asking out of curiosity."

"Why?"

"Well, it has been a long time since I was allowed to play with my food. Have things changed so much?"

Ripper attempted to keep the disgust off his face. The voyeuristic ghoul wasn't something he wanted to deal with right now. He sure as fuck wasn't going to inform Tasha of Epoch's newly developed kink. Ripper was going to have to keep a closer eye out for him.

"Why don't you talk to Ennis about this?"

"She tells me to keep it in my pants, and I should find a male friend to speak about these things."

"Then find one," Ripper blurted out and instantly regretted it when blue eyes turned cloudy. Who would have known vicious man-eating creatures were sensitive?

"I'm not allowed to leave Ennis without a chaperone."

"Maybe if you promise only to play with a female and no attempt to pull a praying mantis act on her or him, I'll chaperone you at Revenge."

"Really?" Epoch let out one of his patented too excited squeals and happy dances.

"Yeah, actually, why do you act like that? Shouldn't your kind be fiercer or something."

"It gives our prey a false sense of security. Although, my kind tends to be more handsome in their human forms than me. The cute thing has never worked in my favor."

"I'm sure. You better go before Ennis starts looking for you."

"She's asleep until the sunsets and then she'll begin to prepare for her evening. Until she leaves for work, she won't look for me."

"You're just full of excuses."

"Is Amora sleeping?" Epoch asked.

"Stay away from my mother's room."

"Oh hi, I didn't know we had another visitor. A friend of yours, Ripper?"

"Yeah, Lark, this is Epoch." From the look on Lark's face, he knew Amora had told her about Epoch.

"Well, can I get you something to drink? We don't have anything to your particular tastes around here."

"I don't want to be a bother."

Epoch practically preened under Lark's attention. It was more than a little disturbing.

"No bother at all, how about some tea? I was going to make Meadow some chocolate milk and get her some cookies."

"Chocolate milk, cookies, could I, um—" Epoch blushed.

"Come on. There's enough for both of you." Lark waved the male over, and Ripper shook his head. "Have you cleaned my couch yet?"

"I'm on it, Mom. Epoch kind of distracted me."

"Don't blame it on him. Epoch, did you still want a snack?"

Ripper cringed at her question and observed Epoch skipping across the room.

"What kind of cookies?"

"Well, there's chocolate chip as I said, but I made some Peanut butter and also some Snickerdoodle. You can have your—"

Ripper blocked them out and went about cleaning up the mess Lark said he'd made. He had a stepmom admonishing him for getting cum on the couch while she offers a cannibal milk and cookies. Fuck, what he wouldn't give for a bit of normal or whatever normal a Jackyl could get.

CHAPTER 12

"Tasha, is there something you'd like to share with the class?"

Tasha rolled her eyes at Lola's teasing voice as five curious faces popped into the mirror. She was attempting to clean the cover-up from the hickey from Hell that graced her shoulder. Concealing it had taken forever. "Have you finally let Baby Boss into those panties?"

"Why would y'all ever think such a thing?" She threw the makeup wipes in the wastebasket beside her dressing area.

"Oh, we don't know, except when he walked in the room earlier you dropped props and blushed liked a teenage girl. Also, if—" Eden grinned and tapped the mark of the twin bruises. "I'm not mistaken. These are fang marks and its common knowledge that our handsome Ripper wouldn't let anyone else do that."

She wanted to ask Eden what she meant but figured it would just throw gasoline on the raging gossip fire.

"Stop, it's none of your business, Ladies."

"We beg to differ, that is the finest Grade A beef ever to grace this place, not to mention he's Amora's son, wealthy, powerful, and from that ridge that's always down his thigh, incredibly well-hung."

Okay, that caused her face to blaze as she shifted, she was still tender from what happened upstairs. Gods, but the male became even bigger when he changed a bit.

"Tasha, you can't keep that to yourself. I did notice she may have been walking funny earlier."

"Oh my god, Sierra, stop. Yes, I am sort of seeing Ripper, that's all you're going to know." She dissolved into laughter as the five grown ass women squealed like teen girls.

"How's the sex?" Lola sighed as made a swooning drop into a nearby chair. "I've heard rumors he's part snake, what's his tongue like?"

Memories of the way his tongue filled her as he'd tickled her g-spot with the tip crashed into her and her thighs clenched. She hadn't realized she'd moaned until the Ladies started laughing.

"That good, lucky bitch."

"I'm out of here." Tasha escaped.

She threw on a jacket over her tank top and grabbed her bag. The Ladies teased her until Tasha exited the dressing room and strode down the hall to the back door. Usually, she wouldn't think about leaving that way, but she wanted to avoid a scene.

What happened earlier wasn't what she'd expected. They were just supposed to talk. She wanted to make sure about—Tasha's face flamed. She shook her head and adjusted the shoulder strap of her backpack on her shoulder.

The stench of trash and faint hints of piss made her nose crinkle. Exactly why she never left through the alley exit. She knew the Ladies meant well with their teasing, but she was still confused about what was happening between Ripper and her. Human and hybrid, would they even have a life together. He would stay the same as she aged normally.

Her head jerked around, casting a look over her shoulder as she felt that prickling sensation at the base of her skull. Searching the shadows, Tasha quickened her steps.

Suddenly she felt trapped in a cyclone, the whipping of the wind around her took her breath, and she tried to scream. The sound of it in her head was drowned out by a roaring in her ears.

Nails ripped at the steely arms that surrounded her as she felt the weightlessness. Her terror-stiffened muscles barely reacted, yet still, she futilely fought against whatever had her imprisoned. Her wide eyes lifted to catch sight of gray flesh stretched tight over harsh angles. Slobber hung in thick, clear ropes from jagged teeth. Bright yellow eyes shined with an intense, nearly tangible hatred.

The beast bellowed seconds before she felt herself plummet to the ground. Pain ricocheted through her body by the force of her fall. Her head throbbed where it had hit the ground.

Her vision swam as what she saw next fought with reality. A huge snake constricted around the thing who attacked her. The chilling rattling sound echoed off the narrow walls of the alley.

She knew it was Ripper. His entire body was elongated and massive in the form she'd only seen hints of in the past. She scrambled back until she pressed to the nearest wall ignoring the wet sludge that soaked her clothes. Hisses and screams, it was all slashing claws and ripping teeth. Ripper flew through the air, and she tried to call out as they charged. His tail arced out, and there was a crackling in the air as flesh met and the enormous gray body connected with a wall. Bricks cracked, the mortar was a whisper of sound as it flowed to the ground.

The fight never seemed to end as they battled blow for blow. Skin split under lethal claws and flesh gave with a sickening sound. Ripper coiled tight around the slightly smaller creature, and the cracking of bone made acid burn at the back of her throat.

Words which had no meaning to her passed between Ripper and the stranger in rapid-fire succession. Her boyfriend's tone condensed into a ragged hiss of rage that sent a cold chill over her skin that summoned goosebumps.

She didn't know what to do, too frightened to move. She gasped as with a flick of his wrist; he sent the creature flying through the air. There was a bright explosion of light, and then it was gone.

"Why, why did you let—" Tears started streaming down her cheeks as she surged to her feet and threw herself into Ripper's arms.

He stiffened before he twined his arms around her. She hid her face in his broad chest. His body coiled around hers, and instead of being terrified, she took comfort in the tight hold of his demon form. The slightly bumpy textured skin under her palms was cool.

"Baby, are you okay?" When he spoke, it was an odd mixture of Ripper's gruff voice and the hiss of a snake.

"I, I think so, I was more frightened than anything." Her heart was still pounding in her ears and adrenaline coursed through her veins. "How?"

"I heard you scream and felt your fear."

She faintly realized that they were moving in a strange fluid zigzag across the alley.

"Here, hold onto this and close your eyes."

Automatically she grasped her backpack to her chest and closed her eyes. A strange shifting of air, a weightlessness not unlike when the demon or whatever grabbed her. Tasha wanted to open her eyes, but she kept them closed as she relaxed completely into Ripper.

"You can open them now."

When her lashes fluttered open, she was home standing in the middle of her apartment. "What the fuck?" She shot a smiling, demon Ripper a shocked glance.

"Demons have perks, one of them is never having to pay for airfare."

"Ha, ha. What the hell happened back there?"

He made no attempt to change, only coiled his lower body tighter and crossed his arms.

"Does it bother you? When I can, I spend a lot of time like this. I'm strangely comfortable."

Defensiveness rolled off him as if he was waiting for her disgust.

"Ripper, I don't mind."

His thinned lips pulled into an off half-smile. To be honest, even though he didn't look like Ripper now, it was alright. His upper body looked human, well, except for the profoundly muscled ridges with onyx and emerald skin stretched over them. Deadly black claws at the end of long, slender fingers.

What fascinated her the most, maybe it should be the eight-foot lower body with a huge rattle at the end of his tail, but, no, it wasn't that. It was his face, lean, yet somewhat rounded lines of his features. Smooth skin graced where dark blond hair normally was, no ears and his nose was flat to his face. "You're beautiful." And he oddly was.

"I thought you'd change your mind when you saw me."

There was plenty of time to question the despondency in his tone later, right now, she needed to know what happened in the alley.

"No, but I need to know what's going on."

"There's a lot to share. I'm just going to hit the highlights and explanations."

She nodded as she sat on the arm of her sofa.

"Lark approached Amora a year ago wanting my mother to rescue her sister. That much you know. The cult Lark escaped from is called The Order of Angelus."

"Angelus, isn't he?"

"The one and the same, he's a Soul Collector, the name is pretty self-explanatory. He feeds off souls to continue his existence."

Did that mean Ripper would one day do the same or did he already?

"Will you?" The question was inadequate, but she'd worked among the supernatural for a long time, and she realized there was much she didn't know.

"Once Angelus returns to where he crawled from or is destroyed, I have to take his place. It's the role that we were created for."

"Why? I know I sound stupid. To realize how little I knew about the people I've lived and worked around for so many years makes me feel naïve."

"Angelus' creator wanted absolute control, unfathomable power. What better way than to trick a human out of their soul. These souls were incapable of resisting the Creator's will, and they served another purpose."

Tasha waited, a shiver seemed to move over Ripper, and he constricted his body tighter to suppress it.

"They fed Angelus. Unfortunately, that was the Creator's downfall. He brought forth the most powerful demon, and when Angelus was able, he killed his Creator and became unstoppable. The only positive is that Angelus has limited time topside, he grows weaker every day."

"How long?"

"Decades, centuries, maybe Millennia, it's tricky, he was the first of his kind. The problem is, I can feel the strengthening of my demon. It could be a gradual transfer of power. Unfortunately, Kali was the first of his kind, so there's a lot we still don't know about what he's capable of doing. He's sure as fuck not going to give away more information than needed, especially if it's going to lead to his death or banishment."

"Why does he hate—" She flinched at his cold chuckle.

"Demonus and Amora fucked up his plan."

"How?"

"They had me. Oh, he wanted that to happen, my birth prophesized. That's another story I'll tell some other time. His plan was to breed Amora and Demonus, and then he was going to take me. Killing Amora was his plan, but they fucked that up by keeping me as far away from him as possible.

"When she went to rescue Meadow, she was captured, and it wasn't the first time. The Order was sent to kill Amora's family when she was a child. They killed her parents and burned the house down with her siblings inside. Imprisoned for nearly a century before she escaped and killed them all in the process."

"Oh God." It was so much to take in. The more Ripper revealed, the stupider she felt.

"She and Angelus have been fighting ever since. After we came back from the last mission to Ireland, I discovered rumors Nicolette, one of Amora's sisters, may have survived the fire. We got confirmation that she did."

"Where is she?"

"Don't know, there's a slave trade, creatures sold as pets or sex slaves. She may have been sold shortly after the fire. I needed information, so I met with someone, and it got back to Angelus somehow. I needed to be taught a lesson, and he sent one of his assassins after you. I'm sorry." Silky smooth palms held her cheeks, but she hadn't even seen him move. "I would never put you in danger."

She stiffened as his lips, cool and firm, touched hers. Tasha felt his shoulders slump. This creature didn't look like Ripper, but it was him. The sense that she hurt him hit her hard. Draping her arms over his shoulders, Tasha kissed him. A gentle melding of lips as she felt his body shift and curl around her. The pressure was tender and comfortable.

Leaning back to study his features, she lifted her hands to trace them with her fingertips. "I know I'm not going to win any beauty pageants."

"Shut up." He opened his mouth to protest, and she slammed her lips to his. Pushing her tongue inside, the extended length of his slithered over hers tickling her palette. She couldn't hold back a moan.

He groaned as he squeezed her tighter. The ripping of fabric as her clothes were reduced to rags barely registered as that sweet and sour flavor exploded on her tongue. She pulled back and licked her lips. "What is that?"

"Venom, deadly to all but my mate. It heightens pleasure as if all your nerve endings are brought to the surface."

The tips of his claws stroked her nipples, and she arched. It felt incredible, beyond anything she'd ever experienced before. She passed by all rational thought or inhibition.

"Ripper, I've never..." She shuddered.

"I've needed you for so long."

Tasha didn't doubt his words as heat flared in his green eyes. A large knot swelled against her lower belly. Her eyes skittered downward, and her breath caught. The ruddy, heavily veined cock pushed from a slit in his charcoal striped belly.

She stroked her fingertips lightly over the smooth skin. He hissed as his body jerked. The musical sound of his rattle intrigued her. Tasha's workout pants disappeared as quickly as the rest of her clothes had.

"Wrap those gorgeous legs around me." Ripper roughly whispered the command against her mouth. "He's been dying to fuck you, taste you." She gasped as his split-tipped tongue flicked over her lips.

Hands stroked up her back and curled over her shoulders, and she barely nodded before he impaled her on his dick. She bit her lips to stifle the scream-moan hybrid. Her cunt was on fire from the stretch, so tight she felt every pulse and jerk inside her.

"So good." Tasha whimpered as she lifted her hips then rolled back down with a hard shudder.

The pleasure was so intense she couldn't breathe.

"Open your eyes."

Tasha forced her heavy lids open at the minute uncertainty she heard.

Tasha breathlessly whispered his name as she stared into his eyes. Maybe it was a figment of her imagination, but he watched her lovingly. He gave her control, she sensed it, and she rode him in slow, steady movements. The moment was fleeting, she knew Ripper and his demon would take over, she just wanted to enjoy her relaxed rhythm a little longer.

His hands touched her everywhere, and he cocooned her with his body. The rough texture of his rattle stroked down her spine and then upward. The strange carnality arched her body and forced her body into a deep backward arch. Firm lips enclosed one aching peak and claws tickled over the other. Her eyes opened wide as she landed on his chest.

Ripper moved with fluid grace beneath her as he smiled and caressed her widespread thighs. He nudged her cheek with his and turned her head. His tongue teased her ear. "Ride me."

A soft tilt pulled at her lips as she braced her hands on his chest and pushed upward. Shifting her hips from side to side, Tasha moaned as his thick cock dragged inside her tight sheath. The pleasure rocketing through her was nearly unbearable as she tried to calm herself.

No other lover ever made her feel as Ripper did. Settling her weight on her knees that barely reached the floor, she started a slowly building lift and fall; grinding when she'd taken him entirely. The heaviness of her breasts swayed as her tempo increased until she was taking him fast and hard. Tasha watched him from under lowered lashes, his mouth was open and his fangs bared.

He groaned and hissed, trembling under her rhythm. Her pussy constricted and her cream coated her inner thighs. It made gripping his body impossible. She heard the score of nails into hardwood.

"Touch me. I can't…" Her pace faltered, and large, strong hands seized her hips in a bruising grip. The push and pull as his arms flexed setting a punishing pace.

Digging her nails into his chest for purchase as her pleasure was so great that it held her suspended. Tasha was unable to fall, to find her release, only pushed higher. Sweaty bodies slammed together with wet, dirty sex sounds. The slap against her clit made her eyes roll, and she tried to close her thighs to ease the sensation.

"No! Open them."

"I can't, it's too good, make me cum. Please!" Ripper's body curled up, and his lips brushed hers. The strain on his face was evident as he stared at her with eyes burning with desire.

"Touch yourself."

She desperately pushed one hand between them, she almost screamed as her fingertips connected with her clit. His pace never faltered, and he swelled larger. Tasha panicked as she tried to fight, escape.

"No, baby, we need this," Ripper hissed. "You're ours, only ours. Fuck," he groaned. "Your pussy feels so good, so, fucking tight."

"Ripper!" She stroked her aching bud frantically.

"Gonna fill you so full. You like when I cum inside you?" The words broken fragments, shattered by groans and curses. She answered him with a jerky nod. "Say it."

His command was a bellow against her mouth.

"Yes, Gods, yes." Tasha's orgasm forced its way through her. Her body bowed forward as she clutched him tight, nails digging into his back. A warm spray exploded between them as she ground against the agony of her release. Pleasure bordered on pain, and she became lightheaded.

Just as Tasha felt the pleasure couldn't soar any higher, Ripper threw back his head and shot deep inside her. She felt every spurt and pulse making her come again in a brutal tensing of muscles. She collapsed onto Ripper's chest as he fell back and his hands stroked in soothing motions over her back.

The air around them crackled with energy as she gasped for breath and prayed her heart would return to normal. Ripper returned to his human form, but remained firm and buried deep inside her. There was a strange heat burning low in her belly as he continued to jerk against the abused walls of her pussy.

"I think you broke me." She groaned the words to his chest.

"Baby, I'm not moving anytime soon. I love you." His lips brushed against the top of her head, and she tried to lift up to meet his eyes, but she was too weak to move. "You don't have to say it, one day maybe."

She felt her eyes burn as she heard the hurt in his voice. Licking her lips, she parted them, yet nothing came out. Tasha nuzzled her cheek to his chest. Tasha hated hurting him, but that stubborn part, the one fighting the truth wouldn't allow her to speak. Ripper wanted her, saw her as his mate and where did that leave her?

Growing older and Ripper moving on, the thought broke her heart.

"You think too much, sleep, we'll talk later." She nodded unable to speak or resist the exhaustion pulling at her. Most of all she needed to avoid the discussion of their future and how impossible that future was.

CHAPTER 13

*L*eaving Tasha sleeping on the bed, he flashed to the outer gate of Angelus' compound. He smiled coldly at the guards through the bars of the gate. The depths of rage that tore at the tenuous restraints of his control caused his demon to ripple beneath his skin. Ripper inhaled the stench of their fear, and his lips thinned to a lethal tilt at the reflexive twitch of fingers around the useless weapons in their hands.

Their permission wasn't needed for him to enter. He would rip the gate down and walk in without a thought. Security was more an act of concealment and determent than for guarding. His fangs dropped, and he felt them flinch just as the grind and rattle of the gate opening broke the tense silence.

Angelus would pay for what he had attempted when sending an assassin after Tasha as a warning to Amora and him. Gravel crunched under his heavy boots as he strode slowly toward the main house. The air crackled around him as he broke through the barrier into his grandfather's realm. His skin prickled with a sense of being watched, scents of demons and shifters floating upon the breeze.

They didn't conceal themselves; they knew he would know they hid in the shadows. He wasn't naïve, and he was aware that they would attack with the least amount of provocation. As much as Ripper was spoiling for a good fight, he had more important matters to tend to. Kali could throw whatever he wanted at Ripper or Amora, but Tasha was human, defenseless against the monsters that could come for her.

His eyes cast from side to side, stopping here and there to alert the bastards he knew they were there. Arrogance was a death sentence, Ma taught him human or not, you never underestimate your opponent, a human could fight as dirty as any demon or were.

As he ascended the creaking steps, he growled at a fresh rush of fear and the stronger smell of rage. Good, he hoped Angelus was pissed. The old bastard knew nothing of controlling his temper. A deceptively wizen old man opened the door with a huge smile on his face. "Cecil, I see you're still kissing the old man's ass."

"If you only paid as well, I would just as easily kiss yours."

Ripper chuckled and embraced the tiny man. It was only a joke. Kali acquired Cecil's soul a long time ago—one of the bastard's first.

"One of these days, Cecil." He stepped back and looked into twinkling eyes. Looking at the diminutive male, you'd never know the dangerous creature existing beneath the helpful façade.

"And I honestly look forward to the day. Angelus has been pacing since you sent his messenger back with his tail between his legs."

"He should know better. You don't mess with what's mine. Angelus in his office?" Cecil stepped to the side and motioned in his with a wave of his arm and a bow. "Eww, Cecil, let's wait for the subservient bullshit until I take over."

"As you wish, Master Ripper."

Ripper rolled his eyes and walked deeper into the house. This was the first time in a hundred years he'd visited, and this time like the last wasn't a social call.

Without knocking he opened the sliding wooden doors and found Kali sitting calmly behind his desk. It was all an act, a show of superiority and it amused him that Kali had yet to learn it didn't work with him. He stepped into the room and closed the doors behind him.

"Ripper, what a lovely surprise." Kali's voice dripped with disdain and the fiery rage burning in the old demon's eyes the worst of all tells.

"I'm sure. You want to tell me about the bullshit you pulled."

"Whatever do you mean? I only sent a messenger to meet your precious Tasha, and I've spoken with him about his overly enthusiastic delivery."

"Is that what it was, a message and what was the message he was delivering?"

"A welcome to the family of sorts, as your mate she'll serve at your side. Your mother has poisoned your mind with these notions of freedom, especially that of women. You must keep that whore of yours on a leash. A stripper? Ripper, could you not do better?"

Lips pulled slowly into a smile, and he felt the fury emanating in waves from the male. "For your information, she's a Burlesque performer, not a whore and putting my mate on a leash is a no, I like my balls right where they are." The calmness of his words belied his fury, and his control held tight by the enjoyment of Kali's loss of control.

"I've had enough of your disrespect!" A fist came down on the desk, the wood cracking beneath the strain.

This was a battle of wills Ripper wouldn't lose. Angelus may be powerful, and that power passed down to him, but no one was more cold and calculated than Amora; he'd learned his lessons well. Lazily crossing his arms over his chest, he observed his grandfather with a bored smile.

"Angelus, you're not going to win. Stay away from my family."

"What family? That dyke mother of yours, the weak father, and that bitch mate."

Ripper lifted a brow. "I will only warn you once."

"You're nothing more than a child, Ripper. I could forgive you and accept you. Don't you want to rule as a Kali?"

"No, the last name is Medina-Jackyl, nothing you ever offer or threaten me with will tempt me. You're desperate and grasping at a crumbling ledge. Fading each day and one day this bastard half-breed will rule your empire."

Killing the demon seemed a viable and pleasurable option, but he held tightly to his control. As with any bully never concede, only fight or push back when necessary. What he'd done to his mate was inexcusable, yet Ripper needed to bide his time.

Ascension at this point was unimaginable. He wanted more time, an aspect of normalcy and time to win his mate over.

"I can deny you the privilege."

Kali's words stunk of falsehoods and Ripper merely grinned pissing off his grandfather further.

"You can't deny me shit, old man. It'll happen whether you want it to or not. It's my right and whether I accept the fact doesn't matter it's my fate, as it's yours to die painfully. Amora will relish the day. Remember, don't fuck with my family again. Next time I might not kill you, but you know I can make you wish for it. I'm well aware I'm the only one who can, and I'll do it with a smile on my face."

"Get out. If you're not here to accept your place, our discussion has ended."

"Very well, but don't forget just what the Medina-Jackyl's are capable of and that we'll bring your entire false kingdom down around you."

The sound of Angelus' growl dissipated as Ripper closed his eyes and felt the shift as he headed for Amora's and instantly regretted it.

"Wow! Um..." He spun and put his back to the origami position Amora had Lark in, and he rolled his eyes. "I'm going to have to learn to call first. Can we talk, Ma?" His mother growled at Lark's high-pitched giggle turned squeal as he heard the sound he was sure a hand connecting with an ass.

Ripper listened to the clank of a buckle and feet scurrying toward the bedroom. "I thought you were staying at Tasha's? You took off after her when we closed."

"Angelus sent someone for her."

"What the fuck do you mean sent someone for her?"

Ripper turned just as she pulled a t-shirt over her head and the rage in the baring of fangs and her eyes made him flinch. His eye twitched, and he laughed covering it with a cough.

"Ma, could you not look like you're rocking a cock please?" Amora's brows rose, and she looked down.

"Shouldn't have fucking showed up without calling." He choked as she reached down and adjusted the length down her thigh.

"Ma, was that necessary?"

"Makes it less noticeable and once you leave, that woman of mine is bent right back over." She smirked, and he groaned.

"How I turned out as well-adjusted as I did is a fucking mystery." Ripper turned, walking into the kitchen and throwing open the fridge.

"Son, you're not going to be here long enough for a snack, get to fucking talking. She's in there keeping it nice and warm for me."

"And we could have stopped there, my stepmom's masturbatory preparation for sex is not knowledge that I want to possess." They needed to work on some boundaries.

"You're my Spawn, haven't you learned a damn thing in all these centuries?"

"Very true." He slammed the fridge door and leaned his shoulder against it. "Angelus sent a demon with a message, but he failed to deliver it because I got to the alley. I sent the messenger back to Angelus with his tail between his legs and took Tasha home."

"And I know you didn't let an attack on Tasha go."

"Ma, I'm your Spawn." He laughed as she smiled proudly. "I went to the compound, and we had a nice talk."

"He still of this world?"

"For now, he's going to make himself a huge nuisance, and I need you to stay on guard with Lark and Meadow. Angelus won't hesitate to try to fuck with them."

Ripper hadn't spoken with Amora about his visit with Dominic, and he didn't plan to yet. The warnings about Meadow worried him, and he needed more information. A trip to Selena and possibly taking the little girl with him. If she was what the old demon claimed, then Selena was in the best position to train her.

"I'll put my people on guard, a call to the pack won't hurt either.

Seamus has his mate and pup to think of, not counting the rest of the pack."

"Tasha is going to fight it, but I have to go out of town to check a lead on Nicolette, and I need you to watch her. I can't focus knowing she's in danger. If I could take her with me, I would, but I can't risk her."

"Your mate will be safe here. Before you leave for wherever, bring her here. I know you want to give her a proper goodbye. Have you explained everything to her?"

Ripper shook his head to answer Amora's question. There was so much he needed to tell her; explain what it meant to be his mate.

"I will explain before I leave, there's a lot too." He needed to have a long talk with Demonus and how best to handle this. Being a Jackyl was too fucking complicated sometimes.

"Be sure you do, Tasha knows and accepts that our kind is out there, but she's not completely versed. Make sure she understands before she no longer has a choice in whether she wants to belong or not. Unless it's already too late."

"Quit hinting at grandkids. She hasn't even let me claim her yet."

Amora stepped close and poked him in the chest. "Don't be that demon, don't be some freakish fuck and dirty little secret." He lifted a brow.

"Ma, where has that finger been?"

"You and your jokes get the fuck out of my house. Lark's probably already done. I'll just have to work her back up again."

"And I'm gone, I'll call tomorrow."

Amora turned and waved over her shoulder as he took a deep breath. He appeared back at Tasha's and found her still asleep. Leaving her for an unknown span of time made his demon claw to get out.

It was always the same over the years. Every time he left and denied himself the claiming, it was excruciating. Stripping, he slipped into bed beside her, curved his arm around her waist and tugged Tasha flush against him. Scooting back, she mumbled his name. He knew he wanted more than his mate was willing to give yet and it didn't stop him from hoping.

CHAPTER 14

Tasha seethed as she stood to the side listening to Amora and Ripper speak as if she wasn't in the room. She wasn't some little woman to be protected. She turned away from the pair, crossed the room and came to stand in front of the window. She'd awakened to find Ripper's arms around her.

His splayed hand had rested low on her belly, and something in the gesture made her uncomfortable. For years she'd been alone, rarely did a man spend the night. The intimacy of it, she felt lost, and she had so many questions she needed Ripper to answer.

"They only have the best intentions, Tasha."

Turning her head, Tasha met the kind eyes of Lark and returned the beaming smile.

"I've taken care of myself for a long time. Okay, I know I'm not used to all this. They make me feel like a child."

"Welcome to my world. Our mates are overly protective."

"I don't want protection." Tasha sighed and rubbed at an aching in her stomach. "He doesn't want me. I can't..." She fell into silence as she turned back to the night scene playing out on the street below. People weaved through the packed sidewalks. Drinks in their hands, laughter blending with music. They were oblivious to the real battles playing out; creatures evolved in life and death struggles.

"Whether you accept it or not, he's yours in every way, and if you would just take the time and truly look, you would see that. Quit trying to see everything through a haze of doubt caused by whatever past you came from."

An arm slipped around her waist, and Lark's slightly shorter body leaned into her side.

"It's not that easy. I don't know if I can accept it." She tensed as she sensed Ripper behind her. His scent, the strange warmth of his body, her every sense knew him.

"Excuse me?" Lark gave her a comforting squeeze and left her alone with Ripper.

"I don't want to hear it. I don't need a damn babysitter. Remember I'm a grown ass woman, I can take care—"

"Stop!" She slowly turned as she heard that strange hiss that only his demon could produce.

Memories of the early morning slammed into her, and his pupils narrowed. Couldn't she hide anything from him?

"I know, but this isn't some human mugger, this is a powerful demon whom I doubt would hesitate to hurt you to get to me. Look at what he's already done."

"You said you spoke with him."

"That doesn't matter. This vendetta isn't going to end after centuries just because I throw one warning at him. I have to find Amora's sister, or at least have proof she died. I don't want to do this, family matters and whether you believe it or not you're part of that. How many times do I have to say how I feel before you'll fucking trust me?"

Tasha dropped her chin to her chest as his body seemed to slump and he placed his hands on his hips. Why couldn't she say it? She'd loved him for so long, and the words wouldn't come.

"I don't know," Tasha mumbled and caught a slight movement as Ripper started to reach for her. He stopped, and she wrapped her arms around her stomach.

"When I come back we'll talk, I promise. If you decide you want me to leave, then that's what I'll do."

She wanted to scream that she didn't want him to go, not now or in the future. Instead of blurting them out, she bit down on her lip and nodded.

The feeling he was about to say something passed as Amora stepped up. "Tasha, we'll be fine, right? Ripper can do his thing, and you'll be safe here with us until he comes back."

"Sure, I'll be the good little mate and keep the home fires burning and all that bullshit." Inwardly she flinched at the harshness of her words, but outwardly she shrugged it off.

"Tasha." Ripper's pain-filled voice broke her heart, but she turned away.

"I'll be fine, just go."

She turned away from the others and went back to staring out the window. Why did she feel the need to push him away? So many questions and doubts, and not a one close to being solved.

A soft breeze surrounded her and then he was gone. "Ripper might be a lot of things, Tasha, but he's my son. You can act like a bitch and push him away all you want. But how long do you think he's going to stick around when he thinks his mate, the one person destined to be his, doesn't give a fuck about him?"

"This has nothing to do with—" Cool fingers caught her upper arm in a hard grip and spun her around. Eyes black and furious bore into hers, and she realized her mistake.

"Listen, little girl; it has everything to do with me. My son's child is resting all warm inside that belly of yours. Ripper might be too worried about keeping his family safe to notice. I'm not."

Tasha gasped as her hand fell to her stomach and the strange ache made sense. "How?"

"Do I need to school you in the way babies are made?"

"No jokes, when?"

"I don't know when, but he or she is there. Barely a heartbeat. What's it going to take for you to realize my son loves you?"

Her eyes burned, and she tried to pull her arm from Amora's grasp.

"Amora, let Tasha go. Your anger isn't going to help."

Black eyes faded to blue as Lark stepped to Amora's side and stroked her palm across her mate's cheek. The love in Amora's eyes had Tasha breathless. Had anyone ever looked at her like that? Did Ripper? Amora's grip eased, and she stepped back to rub the soreness away.

"I'm really—" She felt the heat of a single tear trailing down her cheek as she thought about the implications. A dream long buried, Tasha thought about having a husband and a family. She'd treat her children better than her parents had her.

"Your scent has changed, and there's the faintest beat. If you're not going to give yourself wholly to Ripper, don't fucking stick around and don't tell him. He's waited a long time for you to shed your armor."

"How can you tell me that? Do you think I'm that fucking cruel, Amora?" The questions increased in pitch from low to a squeak; the insult hurt.

Amora was her friend and boss, or until that moment she'd thought so. Tears flowed, and she lost the battle to keep in the quiet sobs. Strong arms embraced her, and she buried her face in the vamp's chest.

"My boy has always known what his fate will be, the role he has to play one day. His life hasn't been easy, Tasha, he's fought and killed. I instilled family is to be protected. He's torn between duty and what he needs." Amora's voice a quiet whisper as her hands stroked Tasha's back. "He needs you, you're his family, but he doesn't need the added pressure of fighting you and his enemies. If you love him, want a life with him and my grandspawn, then quit fucking fighting him. That boy of mine is loyal."

"No one has ever wanted me beyond a few fucks. Ripper's never been very discriminating."

"Tasha, have we forgotten he's my kid and he's a male?"

Tasha smiled at the sardonic tone.

"There's a lot to be discussed, and it isn't my place to bring up. Just know this, Ripper is going to have Hell ahead, and he's going to need someone that's going to stand and fight beside him, not against him."

The woman hugged her, then stepped back. Cool fingertips touched her chin and lifted until she met Amora's gaze.

"I'm sorry." She was. When had she turned into such a bitch? Ripper had shown her how he felt in many ways over the years, maybe at first, she believed it harmless flirting between friends, but quickly it had turned to something else for her. Lust then love. She hadn't wanted to chance losing him as a friend, but now...

"Darlin', don't apologize to me. When your man returns make it right."

She gasped as Amora stepped to her side and placed a hand low on her stomach.

"I'm telling you right now; it better be a boy. I'd prefer not to make some kid pay dearly for his hormones if he messes with my granddaughter. Do we understand each other?"

"I don't think I have much choice about gender, Amora." The ease with which Amora talked about the baby, would her parents be as understanding about a grandchild.

"I'm taking my mate to bed. Eat and rest. We'll visit a friend soon to check on your health. Not exactly sure how the pregnancy is going to affect you being human and all."

Tasha nodded as Amora stroked her belly once more with a strange smile on her face. A softness took over Amora's expression, a tenderness she'd only ever seen bestowed on Lark and Meadow. Cool lips brushed her cheek and then Amora was leading Lark to the bedroom.

She wasn't hungry, but she was tired, too much occurred since she'd awakened. Emotional turmoil dragging her into exhaustion and she wanted to sleep more than anything. Tasha pressed her hands to her stomach, even afraid, she couldn't keep a grin from forming. Happy and terrified, how the hell was she going to tell Ripper? She crossed the room to Ripper's bedroom and stepped into the space separating the screens.

Meadow was sprawled across the bed with dark curls moving as she breathed through the ones that covered her face. Tasha slipped off her shoes beside the bed and sat down to ease the girl over. The small warm body instantly curled against her side as she stretched out.

Ripper's scent clung to the pillow. Now that she had lain down she was wide awake with thoughts swirling in chaotic patterns. Restlessness prickled her skin as if she needed to do something. Now that she was alone, the guilt for how she'd treated Ripper hit her.

Tasha felt selfish, she didn't understand everything about being Ripper's mate entailed, but she knew his loyalty to his family. If there was even a small chance Amora's sister still lived then he had no other choice than to bring her home. The solidarity of the Medina-Jackyl mother and son had made her jealous, a running comparison between her family and theirs. So many years she'd felt Amora, Ripper and the rest of the Revenge Crew were more family than her own.

The exact moment she realized that she loved her boss' son something changed, terrified of losing the one place she felt at home. Tasha made sure she pushed her feelings away. She found any reason to keep Ripper at arm's length. Gods, how she wanted to give in, shed the fear and allow herself to grab ahold of what she'd always wished for—a family.

CHAPTER 15

*R*ipper kept his head down as he entered the warehouse. The sounds of fists connecting with unprotected flesh and bloodthirsty cheers echoed off the walls. Kyros gave him nothing more than an address. The last day was hell, Tasha had fought him swearing she didn't need protection. Amora stepped in and heightened his frustration when Tasha agreed. She'd barely spoken or looked at him as he tried to tell her goodbye.

Ripper hadn't explained everything to her as he'd planned. Her avoiding his gaze had tightened his chest. All that needed to be pushed aside so he could focus on his mission. Once he finished, there would be time or at least he hoped. He wove through the crowd and came to stand at the edge of the crowd that formed a ring. A beast of a man at nearly seven feet faced an opponent, and she was close to six feet with a leanly muscled build.

Flinching as a giant fist solidly connected with her jaw, yet the woman did nothing more than smirk, and her opponent clenched his teeth. He knew that grin and the deathly cold light in her eyes. That was Amora through and through. She left herself open, and without batting an eye, took several punches to the stomach.

Lifting to her toes, she spun and brought the back of her fist across the solid jaw. The massive fucker's head flew back, and with a howl, he lost his cool and charged.

The woman side-stepped, the shifter's momentum sending him forward and a fist connected with his lower spine. His body arched back, and he spun. The scents of testosterone and adrenaline thickened the air; feminine lust laced among the cries for blood piercing the darkness of the warehouse.

It had to be Nicolette, her hair was nearly black, but the eyes were the same. Not to mention the brutality was too much like Amora's as the woman relished every punch and kick.

The harder they fought, the more blood spilled, and the wider the vamp's smirk became. She barely protected herself, merely tensed her muscles and absorbed the blows. Amora did the same, letting her opponent know how little their supposed superior strength mattered.

Something in him pulled at the reins as she spun and bulky, hairy arms circled and trapped her own to her chest. Ripper wanted to step in; family fought back to back, always. The only thing he could do was clench his fists and then as the woman threw her head back the cracking of bone and cartilage rose above all other sounds. Blood poured from the were's broken nose, releasing her as he fell to his knees.

He smirked as she walked slowly around the male and wiped the back of her hand across her mouth. She completed the circle and stood in front of him. "You had enough?" Her voice low, a husky cold whisper of sound.

The male made his final mistake as he cursed and delivered a sucker punch to her lower stomach. Hissing, she twisted her body and brought her elbow across his face, he roared as his jaw dislocated and teeth flew as he fell bleeding to the floor.

A thin man jogged to the woman, he nearly grabbed her wrist, but one look from her caused a fearful jerk as he jumped a few paces back. As she walked from the ring of bodies, they separated and gave her a wide berth. Blood stained the white of her men's tank, and the jeans hung on her slender frame.

He'd found her, but he needed to know for sure. Taking a step back he followed her; his steps slowed as he observed while she removed the tape from her hands. She was too calm, a dangerous animal before the strike.

"If you're looking for pussy, you're looking at the wrong woman." Her voice never rose but could be heard plainly over the murmur of the crowd that geared up for the next round of fighters. Onyx eyes slowly shifted to ice blue as she watched him over her shoulder.

"Wasn't planning on it. Helluva fight. I'm Ripper." He extended his hand, and she shook her head as she tossed the bloodstained coverings aside. Knuckles were split and raw as she flexed her fingers. Ripper shoved his hands in his pockets waiting for her to answer.

"They lined me up against another amateur. You looking to recruit?"

"No, just in town and thought I'd check out the action. Figured I might try my hand, been awhile since I found a worthy opponent."

"That a challenge, boy?" A cold gaze tracked him from head to toe and back as she turned to face him. "Don't look like much, but I've seen quite a few cute ones be downright nasty."

"My Momma taught me not to underestimate anyone, no matter the species." Her nostrils flared, and her eyes narrowed.

"That isn't all vamp in there."

"No, it's not." The exchange was a give and take, but he wouldn't give her an ounce more information than she gave him.

"Not chatty, I like that, kid. Not many have the balls to approach me." She nodded toward the crowd and grinned. "I definitely give them a reason not to, but you, you walked right up. Since you're new, I won't assume you're an idiot."

"No one here is going to scare me. I know a vamp who would take on anyone in this room with a smile on her face. You remind me of her." No interest shown in her eyes to question him.

"Well, I know there are a few slots open for later fights. Harold is the man to see. He was the skinny guy. More fights mean more money."

Ripper began to notice the thick scars running the lengths of her arms, the abraded flesh scarred over around her wrists and throat.

Faded, barely noticeable, yet still there and the dilation of her pupils warned him she'd spotted him looking.

"Don't get nosy, Ripper. I'm feeling friendly for once."

"It isn't my story to ask."

If this turned out to be Nicolette, he couldn't say the same for Amora. The nosy vamp would push, he grinned, but it might be one nasty fight to watch.

"Strange, people normally like to ask questions."

"I got shit I would rather keep to myself. Let's just say we have an understanding."

"Despite myself, I like you, Ripper."

No tilt to her lips showed no emotion, no truth to her words. It was as if staring at a blank slate. He knew the look well. Amora spent many years with a dead-eyed stare and blood on her hands.

"You'd be in a minority."

He observed her use a bottle of water to get cleaned up. She removed her bloody shirt and tossed it into a barrel jumping with flames. She quickly dressed, white dress shirt and a tie then pulled a charcoal fedora over her shaggy hair. The stranger had yet to give him her name.

"See you around, Ripper, I fight every Saturday night. Next time, Pretty Boy, maybe we can go a few rounds." She slung a backpack over her shoulder.

"Hey, you didn't give me your name?"

"Nico, everyone just calls me Nico."

She waved over her shoulder and disappeared into the crowd. It was her. He fought the urge to call her back. He needed more, proof, something more than wishful thinking. Too simple, to some extent it felt off, and he wasn't ready to jump in. Telling some strange woman that he may be her nephew, especially when she can brawl like Nico, wasn't a smart move.

A week, that's the amount of time he had to gather more intel before he'd be back here.

He wanted to follow her, blurt it out and take her home to Amora. Lark did a lot to bring his mother peace, and soothe old wounds. This female could be Nicolette, her sister, a piece of the family Amora still mourned after centuries, and if Nico survived, maybe the others had as well. The actual question was, how to tell his mother without her wanting to track down her possible sibling?

Ripper couldn't keep the truth from her. She'd suffered too many years with guilt. A little more time, seven more days and he would know more. One mission partially completed, only a few other jobs to finish. Meadow, he needed to know for sure his family was safe at least for now. Selena would help, but he needed more information from Dominic. He'd wait a few days, visiting the old demon alerted his grandfather. The less Kali knew, the better.

Now, he was going home because he had peace to make with his mate. Tasha was the most important at the moment.

CHAPTER 16

The bed bounced, and high-pitched giggles woke her. Tasha turned her head and tried to focus her blurry eyes to the opposite side, and a slow, sleepy smile tugged at the corners of her mouth. Ripper had Meadow trapped as he tickled her sides, a broad smile matched the bright light in his green eyes.

"Oops, Little Miss, we woke someone up." Two wide-eyed gazes turned her way. "G'morning."

Her lashes fluttered closed as Ripper squished a protesting Meadow to lean over to brush a soft kiss to Tasha's lips.

"When did you get home?" He traced her lips with the pad of his index finger, and her heart stuttered.

"A few hours ago." He rolled his eyes as he motioned to her and Meadow. "Found two bed hogs taking up my bed and I had to suffer all squeezed up against the wall." Meadow was grunting and kicking trying to push her big brother up.

"You should have woken me up," she whispered sleepily.

"No, I don't require much sleep, a nap here and there. A call came this morning...we got our house." Her brows quickly rose.

"Ours?"

Ripper nodded and gave her that crooked grin she found sexy as hell. "Yeah, I bought it for us, I can get a different one if you don't like the one I picked."

She shook her head and quietly chuckled as he narrowed his eyes as Meadow landed a small punch to his gut, but he still ignored her.

"No, it's perfect."

She'd never had a house before with no rent to pay, and she'd always wanted to find somewhere she could call home. Ripper wanted that with her, a life, she watched him with Meadow and wondered if kids were included in the plan.

Suddenly she was nervous about telling him, scared about what he would say. Knowing it was silly, Amora instilled a strong sense of family, and the baby would be a part of that. Although she wanted more than duty, he professed to love her and out of all her reservations those were the hardest to let go.

"Ripper, let me up!"

Ripper rolled his eyes and fell to the side. As soon as Meadow was released, she took off. The little girl quieted as she headed for Lark and Amora's room.

"Tasha."

"Ripper." They spoke in unison. "I'm sorry."

He slid across the bed and took her in his arms. "There's nothing to be sorry for. I know this is all strange and hard to accept. I wish—" Ripper sighed and closed his eyes.

"I'm scared."

"What are you scared of? I wouldn't hurt you for anything."

Tasha bit her lip as she took his hand, and as she rolled to her back, she placed it on her lower belly. His eyes widened, and a smile lit up his face.

"Really?" One second the excitement was there and the next panic. "Oh shit, are you okay? Are you sick?"

"Stop, I'm all right, shocked and a little frightened. I thought about it before, you know, the whole kids thing, but I never thought of it as a reality. A close family is something I never had before. I just don't want you to feel—" His mouth slammed against hers taking her breath and words.

Ripper shifted his body and came to rest between her thighs. Tasha instantly became wet, her pussy clenched as the bitter burn of his venom flowed over her tongue. Moaning into his mouth, she twined her legs around his waist.

Ripper's growl vibrated against her lips as the sound of small feet neared. "We need our own place or a room with a door."

"Yucky, they're kissing again!"

Tasha whimpered as he dropped a chaste kiss to her mouth and rolled away.

"I can kiss my wife if I want too, Little Miss."

Tasha laughed as Ripper threw a pillow and Meadow took off squealing.

"Wife?" Tasha arched a brow as she cast a glance at his smiling face.

"You're my mate, the one destined for me and as soon as we can arrange it, Mama will marry us."

"Amora?" Tasha tried to picture Amora acting as minister for a wedding, and something about the image made her laugh. "I can't imagine Amora officiating nuptials."

"Me either, but Medina-Jackyl tradition, the eldest member of the family performs the marriage ceremony. It may only be us remaining of the line, but we want to have as many traditions remain as possible."

"Tell me about—" Family secrets were held tightly by Amora and Ripper, neither spoke of the past. She knew them in this time, and she didn't know how much she could ask.

"Baby, you can ask whatever you want, I can see the look in your eyes, and as honest as I want to be with you, there's a lot that Amora and I regret."

"Like what?"

"Being what we are…" He sighed, and she reached out stroking the roughness of his cheek. "You've seen, we have much blood on our hands."

"Ripper, I won't ask about Amora, but has it always been self-defense to protect your family?" With his eyes closed, he nodded, and she leaned forward to brush a kiss to his mouth. "That's all that matters."

"I want to take you and Meadow somewhere—to meet someone." A shadow moved across his bright green eyes, and she frowned.

"Who?"

"Selena, an old lover of Amora. I have some questions and with the —" A smile curved her mouth as his hand rested low on her belly. "—baby. I would like her to check you. I want to know how having a baby that's part demon and vamp will affect your health."

"Is she the Healer Amora spoke of when she announced I was pregnant?"

"No, she's a witch." Her eyes widened, and he smiled. "It's a long story. It's okay and perfectly safe. You'll love her."

"Okay, I trust you." She turned as she heard Lark softly talking to Meadow in the other room.

"I'm going to speak to Lark about taking Meadow out for the day."

He dropped his head, shielding his gaze from her. There was something he wasn't telling her—she could feel the tension and uncertainty. It was odd and felt like he was in her head.

"I love you," Ripper whispered the words as his arms tightened around her and he buried his face in the curve of her neck where it met her shoulder.

"I love you too."

Ripper pulled back, his hands came up to bracket her face in his strong hands and gently kissed her lips. "I'll leave you to get ready."

Tasha nodded, observed him as he jumped off the bed and disappeared. She lay back on the bed. Her hands came up to cover her face. She wondered what he was hiding. The shadows darkening his gaze tightened her stomach with apprehension. Sadly, she had no choice but to wait.

* * *

GODS, she hated the flashing thing, she placed her hand on her stomach trying to settle the rolling feeling. Ripper opened the door of the shop and walked into the dim interior holding Meadow's hand. An elderly woman stood up from a chair in the corner, but her feeble frame seemed an illusion. She didn't know why she thought it, but there was something deceptive in the stuttered movements.

"Selena."

"Ripper, what a lovely surprise and you brought me your beautiful bride." A voice cracked with age, but her dulled eyes twinkled with mischief. Ripper stepped up and leaned down to kiss the wrinkled, paper thin cheek.

"Tasha, Meadow, this is Selena, a very old friend of Amora's."

Meadow pressed closer to Tasha's thigh as the little girl looked up at the old woman. A cold, twisted smile pulled at the corners of Selena's wrinkle-cracked lips.

"Well, young lady, so much power, a tasty—" A hiss broke through the glazed look the woman cast at Meadow.

"You'll rein in your appetite, Selena, I would hate to kill you."

She shivered at the cold-edged warning in Ripper's voice. Eyes narrowed as Selena seemed to recoil and take a step back.

"That sounded too much like your mother, Ripper. I'm offended by your lack of trust." With creaking bones, the woman eased to her knees.

"Behave, or you won't have to worry about that curse of yours."

Tasha shot Ripper a questioning look and noticed the serpent eyes with their thinned pupils.

"I have encountered few in my extended lifetime with the degree of power in such a small form. Child, does he come to you in your dreams? A man dressed in shades of safety?" A gnarled hand reached for Meadow and Tasha turned pulling the child away.

"Ripper, what's going on?"

"It's okay, I learned something, and I need to know if it's the truth." Ripper moved to the other side of Meadow and knelt to gather the child onto his lap. "Meadow, it's okay, I'll hold you the whole time."

Meadow continued to hold tight to Tasha's hand, but relaxed against Ripper's chest. Skeletal fingers carded through dark curls and eyes rolled upward before they closed. A mere sliver of white peeked from beneath the lowered lashes. Words in a strange language quickly tumbled from Selena's tongue. An odd electrical current emanated outward from Selena, small fingers clenched around hers as that charge lifted Meadow's curls in a frizzy halo.

Meadow gasped, and Tasha started to reach for the frightened child. "Easy, child." The woman's voice changed, her skin became smooth, and silver hair turned a sleek honey-brown. What the hell was going on? Tasha turned her attention to Ripper, but his eyes had closed, and his brow was furrowed.

Would she ever grow used to the strangeness of her mate's life? Tasha knew the man, the same jokingly flirtatious man she'd fallen in love with, yet in such a short time, she learned Ripper and Amora hid so much from the ones around them. The spell broke as the younger version of Selena pulled back and opened crystal-clear azure eyes.

"Ripper, you need to take her and go far away, consecrated ground. He cannot possess her. Kali is power hungry, mad with the need for more. This child will give him exactly what he needs." A hint of panic tinged Selena's voice, a desperation that belied the coldness and hunger before. The woman rolled quickly to her feet and gripped the sides of her skirt. Selena nervously fidgeted, paced in short, quick steps nearly turning in circles.

"There is nowhere I can take her. He'll send someone for her no matter where she is. I'll just have to figure out something else." Tempered rage deepened Ripper's voice, and Tasha automatically reached for him, combed her fingers through his soft hair. He leaned into her caress and rested his cheek on her thigh. "Can you check Tasha and our baby?"

"Of course." Her voice softened, and Selena stopped her turning mid-motion. Tensing as the witch approached and slender hands pressed against her stomach. "Healthy, both are perfect, but I hate to tell you your cravings are going to become odd shortly. Prepare, demon and vampire will push the human DNA aside. Have you ever drunk blood, my dear?"

Tasha swallowed hard as her stomach rolled at the thought. "Um, will that be necessary?"

"You will not have a choice. The demon will need to consume raw flesh, and the vamp needs blood, at some point, she will require both."

Tasha gagged at the knowledge, she knew her baby wouldn't be of the usual, human variety, but she hadn't comprehended the full scope of what it would require.

"You'll be okay. The child will make you crave it, and if you're lucky, your sexy mate can help with the blood. A little feeding during foreplay or during—" Another one of Ripper's growls cut Selena off.

"Selena!"

Tasha listened to the woman cackle as her body shifted back to the unassuming elderly woman. Selena hobbled back to her chair and sat.

"Quit scaring my mate. When it comes time for our child to need more than what Tasha can provide, we will discuss that together. No nasty thoughts from you."

"I was a freak in my day, my dear."

Confusion made Tasha frown at the wistful comment. She hadn't forgotten Ripper had moved the conversation away from Meadow and the weird revelations.

Perplexity made her dizzy, and once again she wondered what she had gotten herself into. Ripper and Selena verbally sparred as she absently stroked Ripper's hair and held Meadow's hand. Tasha found herself lost in her muddled thoughts; sure that whatever their situation was, it would only get worse before it got better. What hell awaited in the days, weeks or months ahead? More importantly, would she still have the family she loved?

CHAPTER 17

Selena's warnings circled in his head days later, although she'd merely confirmed what Dominic said, he now had it from two sources. Telling Amora topped his list, only he hoped to temper the blow with some good news and make it easier for her to take. He flashed outside the warehouse where he'd found Nico and walked inside. His first stop was finding the skinny male that organized the fights.

Ripper was in the mood for a fight, so he pushed through the crowd and approached the man. "Harold?"

"Who's asking?"

"Ripper, is Nico fighting tonight?" Harold's washed out brown eyes lit up with greed and Ripper reached into his pocket to pull out a roll of cash. "I got five grand that says I can take her down."

"You fight in fifteen." A gnarled hand reached out and took the offered bet. Ripper nodded and slipped back into the crowd. He didn't want Nico to see him yet. The moment their eyes connected again would be across a makeshift ring.

A woman like Nico would trust him more after a strenuous battle. His mother judged people on how they handled themselves in the face of adversity. A feeling in his gut said the same about the woman he believed to be his aunt. He removed the leather jacket and hung it from a nail in a dark corner.

He only had minutes to prepare himself, clear his mind of all distractions. There would be blood and broken bones, adrenaline-fueled chaos. The creature he was beneath the surface prickled under his flesh, clawed to get out.

Ripper reminded himself he merely needed to win, his demon would recognize family, and as base as his demon could be, it also put family above all else. It already watched over Tasha and the baby, bonded with her and aware of Tasha's every move and mood. It would feel her fear as strongly as she and this fight was for family.

The warrior took over in the guise of deadly calm. Felt the release of his fangs from his receding gums and small patches of skin changing, shifting to green streaked with black. Ripper removed his t-shirt leaving him bare above the waist. Muscles corded at the ready, he took one last deep breath and headed toward the crowd as they announced the fighters.

As his name rang out, he pushed through the crowd, and his smirk matched Nico's as their gazes met.

"So, kid, we meet again."

"Nico." He nodded, the crowd went crazy as Harold exited the ring of bodies and Nico moved closer. Shots were feigned, each one met with a chiding bored raised brow.

The first quick succession of jabs landed, knocking him back. "Not bad for an old woman, Nico." A front kick took the vamp by surprise. The more blows they landed and blood they shed only made their smirks widen.

"Ready to give it up, Kid, I think you need to develop a larger set before you take me on again."

Ripper struck with lightning quick punches, combinations, right, left, right and uppercut. The scent of blood and sweat, adrenaline and savagery filled the air emanating from the bodies that crowded closer the longer the fight continued.

A give and take, punishing brutality, skin splitting beneath hammering fists and kicks with the force of a semi connecting with unprotected bodies. He ducked the spinning kick as Nico lashed out, Ripper's boot connected with the side of her knee and she collapsed. With a fluid movement, she vaulted from a prone position to fighting stance.

A sneer pulled at the corners of his mouth as his lips thinned and he dropped his arms to the side. Anger flashed as eyes went from blue to black at the insult. A quick combo connected with his contracted abs and his elongated tongue slithered passed his lips as venom dripped from the needle-like fangs. A high, roaring hiss rose above the bloodthirsty cries of the mob as his venom burned away a layer of flesh.

Slender hands gripped his hair and drove his face down as she brought her knee up. He hooked her supporting leg and swept her off her feet. Straightening he stared down at her, and a snarl pulled her lips tight. Pain shattered inside him as he fell to his knee.

"Fuck! Nico, fucking low!" He held his nuts, and she chuckled.

"Give up?"

"Medina-Jackyl's don't give up."

Black eyes widened, and he took advantage of her shock. His punched landed to her mid-section, and she flew through the air, knocking the crowd out of the way like bowling pins. The brick wall gave as she slammed into it and crumpled to the floor.

"You give up, Nico?" Ripper stood in the middle and watched her. "Because I need a fucking drink."

"You're buying."

"I won, you should be buying." She flipped him off, and he laughed as he went to find Harold to collect his winnings.

Thirty minutes later, they set in a dark corner of a bar. He'd followed Nico to the abandoned looking building in the desert. "What's your angle, kid? I won't fall for some con job."

"No con, names Ripper Medina-Jackyl, my mother is Amora, your sister." A muscle jumped under the amp's eye—it was the only outward tell.

"Amora's dead, along with the rest. You wanna change your bull-shit story?"

"Your parents were Samuel and Helena, the Order of Angelus assassinated them. They wanted Amora, the rest of you were expendable. Amora was imprisoned for eighty-seven years before she escaped. She took her revenge in the most brutal ways possible and also tore herself up with guilt for not being able to save her siblings."

"All this time has passed, what the fuck does she want from me?"

"We didn't know you were alive. A woman escaped The Order, and by luck, she stumbled across Amora. Lark asked for my mother's help in rescuing her sister. During the mission, we came across information which said you may have survived. We're hoping that since you did, that the rest did as well."

"Naomi is dead. The last time I saw Bram, he was pinned under a beam. His clothes were on fire, and he wasn't screaming. Damn sure he's dead too. I heard a baby crying when I made my way outside." Eyes clouded and Nico seemed to lose herself in the past. She shook her head and steeled her features. "My newborn brother burned to death when I couldn't get to him. He was still attached by the cord, covered in blood and the ceiling collapsed. I still hear his cries."

Ripper roughly pushed his fingers through his hair. "He could have survived, Amora survived almost a century of hell, they could have too. Amora and I won't stop until we have proof."

"Why is it so important? You don't know us. Fuck, we're just a memory for this vamp you claim is my sister."

"We fight back to back, family sticks together. If finding you gives my mother a little more peace, that she didn't ultimately fail then that's what I'm going to fucking do. Lark, my mom's mate, has eased some of her nightmares, but..." The words wouldn't come, he didn't know how to explain it to the cold woman sitting across from him.

It was like looking at another version of his mother. Haunted gaze combined with the scars he'd seen on her, those all didn't come from fights. Ripper had seen enough scars from torture, especially the ones that graced his mother's pale flesh.

"Very noble and sweet."

"You can mock me all you want, I don't know you and you sure as fuck don't know us. Your opinion means shit to me. All I know is my mother has suffered long enough. What do you lose in taking a chance?"

"What's Amora like?"

That one question fueled a small semblance of hope. The curiosity meant maybe she believed a bit of his story. It was only one phase of the battle.

"Like you. When I saw you fight, the look in your eyes and evil smirk. Taunting an opponent larger than yourself, Amora would and has done the same. She fought out of Hell and survived, possibly not sane, but she made it out."

"What does she do?"

"She owns a bar in New Orleans, Club Revenge, a burlesque club. If nothing else, my Momma loves the ladies. Good thing her mate is understanding."

Nico scrubbed her hands over her face and removed her fedora. Her body seemed to collapse in on itself as she rested her arms on the table. Her indecision shifted and changed in her eyes to something akin to weariness. "Are the others alive?"

"We don't know. Until we laid siege to one of The Order's monasteries, we didn't even know you were alive. I discovered whispers of a Pure-born sold in an underground auction. The rumors were old, and I figured I'd never find you."

She stiffened at the mention of the auctions. He could only imagine the horrors. To be raised as a warrior, proud and strong, to be broken; death would have been kinder. The scars on her wrists and neck explained without words.

"Don't pity me, kid, I don't need it. I survived, and my Master didn't. What happens now?"

"That's up to you, I give you an address, and you make up your mind. If I tell Amora I found you, Nico, you're not going to get a choice. She'll come for you one way or another."

"I have some—" Nico paused. "Business to attend to, it'll take me a week at the most. Give me a week, and I'll be at the address you give me."

Ripper was about to speak as fire tore through his abdomen. His demon was lashing out enraged. Tasha screamed in his head. His claws broke through the surface of the scarred table. Shifting in public wasn't the smartest idea.

"Easy, Kid, control it!" The painful prick of nails breaking through the skin of his forearms brought him down. "What's wrong?"

"Someone has fucked with my mate. I have to go, if they've taken her, I will—" His demon roared and jerked at the reins of his control.

"Family fights back to back, right?" His only answer a stiff nod. "Let's go." With Nico's help they made it outside as soon as the cool desert breeze surrounded them, he wrapped his arm around Nico, closed his eyes and headed for home.

CHAPTER 18

Pain radiated through her head as her eyelids refused to open. Then it all came rushing back. She'd been playing with Meadow in the Club while Amora slept. Lark left to run errands. Like in the alley, an intense cyclone of air knocked her off her feet. Meadow screamed her name. Powerless to do more than grab the little girl and hold on as the world spun. Everything had gone black as nausea twisted her stomach into knots.

Reaching out, she searched for Meadow, but her fingers met only damp, loose soil. As she was rolling to her hands and knees, the agony in her head was threatening to make her vomit yet she searched blindly until her fingertips connected with a tiny sneaker.

"Meadow, baby, wake up." Tasha collapsed next to Meadow's small form. "Meadow, baby, don't, come on, please, wake up for me. Just for a few minutes."

Panic turned her voice shrill as she searched for wounds, finding the tiniest of pulses. She combed her fingers gently through the little girl's tangled curls, and tears began to fall as her hands connected with damp hair and the coppery scent of blood wafted on the air. It blended with the musky molded smell of rotten wood and damp earth.

She repeatedly begged for Meadow to open her eyes, anything, a muffled moan turned briefly to Tasha's name. Soft sobs broke the silence only filled with Tasha's ragged breathing.

"It's okay, Momma Amora and Ripper, they'll find us. Don't worry okay?" She whispered the words against Meadow's ear as tiny arms weakly hugged her neck.

Please let her be telling the truth. Sifting of soil downward followed the heaviness of steps as people moved around above their cell. The longer time dragged, the more worried she became for Meadow. She wouldn't wake up for more than a few seconds. Her sweet voice slurred. Fear gripped Tasha in a chokehold as pains began to shoot through her lower stomach.

Tears flowed hot and freely down her cheeks as she squeezed her eyes shut. Her knees curled upward, and Tasha's heart beat a panicked crescendo of escalating terror. A nervously sung lullaby started as Meadow's sobs began anew and Tasha's cramps intensified. She stiffened at the grind of metal against metal, and the door opened.

Without a single word, fingers twisted in her hair and pulled her to her feet. She desperately held to Meadow, but a severe blow caused a scream as the sound of bones cracking, and her left arm was useless.

"I won't leave her!" Tasha kicked, bit, aimed for their groins just right and they released her. The nails of her right hand clawed at the dirt. Her fight was useless, they kicked her, heavy boots stomping onto her back.

They weren't going after Meadow; it seemed they only wanted her. Tasha rolled to the side and curled into a ball to protect her stomach. The men didn't speak, her vision dimmed, and as she lost consciousness, she faintly felt the new roundness of her abdomen.

* * *

THE POUNDING in her head worsened as she tried to open her eyes. Voices muffled, panicked and confused. "Man down!"

Tasha's limbs tingled with the sensation of pins and needles. When she rolled to her knees, pain cut through her as her arm gave under her weight. She quickly realized her mistake as nausea overcame her. Her empty stomach constricted and she heaved.

Her good hand went to her stomach when a painful gasp pushed past the acid-raw lining of her throat. Fingers searched the new curve. In her panic, she searched her mind for some explanation. It was a subtle fullness, and a faint roll against her palm calmed her. The baby was okay, for now.

The scurrying of feet caught her attention. "What the fuck happened?" They stood over a prone man, and his groans confirmed he wasn't dead.

"He tried to tie the bitch up, next fucking thing I know he's flying through the air."

Her body tensed as the man approached, the air crackled around her and he froze. The man tried to move forward again, but he stopped like he'd hit a wall.

"I'm not talking about her. The girl, we had specific orders not to harm her." Meadow, Tasha's fear amped up, was the little girl okay? She needed to get back to her, the thought of Meadow all alone in the dark cell hurt and terrified spurring her on. Forcing herself to her knees, she cradled her injured arm to her chest.

The men ignored her—their discussion was heated as they argued amongst themselves. Details of Ripper and her discussion, what Selena had told them filled her head. She didn't understand the new course of her life, living with uncertainty as familiar as the sound of her voice, yet so many changes in such a short time.

"Take her back to the girl. I have to summon the Healer to fix your fuck up."

An old door pathetically slammed with a rattle of weakened slats. Heavy boots were mere whispers of sound on the dirt floor. Rough fingers, a grip meant to cause pain circled her upper arm. Agony tore through her broken arm, and her vision became fuzzy at the edges.

She needed to steel herself, prepare for whatever awaited. Being strong for Meadow, and Tasha's hand fell to her stomach, the baby and the oddness of the new contour brought her a small measure of comfort.

"Move!" She flinched at the booming voice as she concentrated on moving her feet, one in front of the other. The walls of the narrow corridor were nothing more than carved out soil and ancient-looking wooden beams.

Claustrophobia threatened to choke her, and she tried to ignore the pain when the stranger behind her pushed her forward when her steps faltered.

"Stop."

Tasha looked around confused as he pushed a door open to her left. The surface was deeply gouged with age and abuse.

She barely stayed on her feet as he threw her into the room. The door closed and locked behind her, and she ran to Meadow. Her tiny frame still in the same position as when they dragged Tasha away, and she fell to her scraped knees.

Hands frantically searched while she whispered, "Meadow, baby, come on, wake up." The blood was dried and crusty in the usually soft curls, but the lack of fresh blood swamped her with relief.

Meadow's skin felt cold to the touch, so Tasha gathered the child to her one armed and sat down to cradle the small body to her chest. Awkwardly she wrestled her t-shirt up and stretched it over Meadow's body, placing her against Tasha's skin. Tears once again burned her eyes at the sound of weak whimpers.

"Amora and Ripper will come for us, I promise, they will be here any minute. You'll be fine. You just have to hold on for me."

She made a sling from Ripper's plaid, button-down shirt. Fighting her fear and pain, her words tumbled out in nonsensical phrases of comfort. Her free hand slowly stroked over Meadow's back, attempting to soothe them both.

They would find them because they had too, Ripper loved her and Amora believed in the family above everything. She just hoped that her mate and Amora found them in time. Meadow shivered, and Tasha curled her body around her as best she could. Keeping the little girl warm was her priority. Lowering her forehead to the top of Meadow's head, she tried to save her strength.

The tiny and unfamiliar movements inside her belly made her

smile wistfully. Tasha tried to picture what her son or daughter would look like, probably like Ripper. Wavy dark blonde hair and crystalline jade eyes, something told her the child she carried was a girl. Would she be like Ripper? She smiled and wondered why the vision of a little snake demon slithering around the house amused her so.

Ripper would spoil his daughter rotten. What would their life be like now? Words softly mumbled against her chest.

"Meadow, what did you say?"

"She's mad." Relief made her sag against the wall, awake was good, it had to be.

"Who's mad?"

"The baby, she's mad, but she's weak." Tiny fingers stroked her bare belly, and she shivered.

"What do you mean she's weak, baby?"

"She's not big...she can't do the flashy thing Ripper does. She's getting tired."

That one little statement nearly stopped her heart. What if something happened, she couldn't bear to lose, no, she refused to think about it. They would be fine, Ripper would find them.

"We just have to rest, just lay down, and we'll take a little nap. Okay, and when we wake up, Momma 'Mora and Ripper will be here. Just sleep." She whispered the words into hair that faintly smelled of baby shampoo under the metallic odor of blood.

She just kept talking, words quiet, telling stories she remembered from her childhood and sang and hummed lullabies. Everyone needs to be okay, Tasha wouldn't survive losing Meadow or the baby. As she attempted to comfort, she barely registered the steady flow of tears wetting Meadow's curls.

CHAPTER 19

*I*t was all wrong, the pain bent him in half, and Nico barely calmed him enough for him to take them to Amora. Legs collapsed as he appeared with Nico in Amora's living room.

"Ripper!" Lark's panicked voice preceded the feel of trembling hands holding his cheeks.

"Tasha and—" He slammed his fists into the hardwood floor as he tried to pull himself together. This wouldn't do, he had to be in control, his mate and child needed him. The anger flared, and he pulled it around him like a cloak as he surged to his feet. A surprised squeak sounded as Lark fell back.

Amora surged forward and helped her mate up, wrapped protective arms around her. "You better fucking tell me what the hell is going on? Where is my daughter?"

"The Order, I felt Tasha's pain, her fear upset our baby, and they called to me," Ripper explained in a fast flowing of words as he tried to control his rage and pain. His, Tasha's and their baby, it swirled together into an agony even his demon never came close to producing.

"Amora?" Nico's uncertain voice, he turned his head to find the sisters staring at each other.

They slowly began to circle each other, their eyes roaming and Lark stepped back to allow her mate and Nico their moment. He nearly broke it up because they didn't have time for it, he needed to find Tasha.

"Nicolette, is—" Ripper nearly stepped forward as Amora's arms shot out and her hands cupped her sister's face. Crimson tears rolled down his mother's cheeks as she pulled the woman forward and her lips pressed against Nico's forehead.

Slender fingers fisted in the back of Amora's shirt. "I thought... you're here, alive." A knot formed in his throat as he watched the newly reunited siblings.

"Alive is a relative term."

He watched Amora slowly search her sister, stroked over the scars at her throat, removed the jacket to find the long-healed wounds on her wrists.

"I should have, I failed, the house was burning, I heard screams, I tried to get away, I promise I did. You, they wouldn't let me go, I fought to get back into—" Words failed them both as tear-dampened lashes fluttered.

They held tight, for centuries he'd watched his mother, the badass vamp destroyed anyone and anything in her path. The only weakness Amora showed was when she lost herself in her past, the nights when screams rang out, and she fought against specters of the Hell she'd escaped.

It was uncomfortable to see the strong woman who raised him reduced to tears and sobs, a weakness he'd never seen her allow. He wanted to turn away, to give them privacy, yet when he did his gaze fell on Lark. The small woman's arms wrapped around her middle, and unashamed, she wept as she watched her mate embrace Nico.

Them together was what he'd wanted, to free her of some of her past, but he knew this was only one piece returned. He needed to find the rest, to bring them home or if not, at least make sure the rest were dead.

Nico and Amora pressed their foreheads together and stared into each other's eyes. His gaze narrowed, some silent message passed between them. Their positions mirrored, knees touched as they sat back on their heels. They seemed lost in the moment as if the world around them no longer existed.

Anger flared, they didn't have time for this, his mate and Meadow needed to be found now. The family reunion could wait, but he couldn't speak and break the moment between them. Centuries of time passed since they had been together, too much time to think and feel alone. Guilt ripping sanity to shreds every time Amora's eyes closed.

No sooner had the moment started it passed, and the two women pushed to their feet. "What happened?"

"I already told you, The Order took Tasha and Meadow, I don't know which was the intended target. It doesn't matter...they're both gone. I can't sense where they are, I know from the fear and sadness they're still alive."

"Would they be stupid enough to take them back to the castle? That would be a sloppy fuck up."

"Do you think they're smart? They follow Angelus with blind devotion. Dominic?"

"I don't trust that old demon, but it seems we have a mutual enemy. It could be in our favor to pay a visit. What aren't you telling me, Ripper? I can see it in your eyes, so don't fucking bullshit me."

"Meadow is psychic, a foreteller of death, I took her to see Selena to confirm it. Angelus plans to use her to amass souls. He's becoming weak. Fading more each day."

He watched Amora as she paced like a caged animal. Rage rolled off her, a tangible aura of hate. Pictures rattled on the walls as he found himself slammed back against the bricks and black eyes bore into his. Amora bared her fangs as she pivoted and he felt weightless as he caught himself before he crashed into a pillar. Crouching as he observed her, muscles rippled beneath the pale skin as she stalked him with a deadly gaze.

"And you didn't bother to tell me?"

"What was I going to say? They should have been safe here, I underestimated Angelus' desperation, and he *is* becoming desperate. He can't be seen as weak or his kingdom will come crashing down."

"What about Nico, how long, Ripper?"

He started to respond, and Nico spoke up.

"He came to me a week ago. I didn't know who he was until tonight. You can't blame him, and this posturing bullshit has got to end. It's not going to get Tasha and Meadow back. Where the fuck do we start?"

Ripper cast a glance at Nico as she slipped off her dress shirt to reveal another men's t-shirt. She wore the same expression Amora did before going into battle. For two women separated for centuries, the similarities were remarkable. The same defensive posture with their arms crossed and always on guard for the next fight.

"Dominic, he's cryptic as fuck, maybe if we get there, I can sense them."

"What if Kali fucked up? What if he has them at the compound? You know that Nico and I can't make it through the barrier."

"Yes, you can, but I don't think he wants them that close especially since he knows we'd come for them. Lark?" He turned his head as a loud sob broke through their planning, and the woman dropped to her knees.

Amora was instantly at her side, and his mother gathered her mate in her arms. They rocked as Amora stroked the woman's back and whispered love and promises, promises she would never make unless she were willing to die to keep them.

"She shouldn't be making promises she can't keep." Nico's voice came from his left, and he turned to look at her.

"Amora will keep them, she'll die for her family and Meadow is her daughter, Tasha carries her grandchild. We'll bring them home, and if not, we'll kill them all." The woman merely nodded and turned, and they stood shoulder to shoulder.

"She shouldn't be left alone while we go? Is there somewhere she'll be protected?"

"Seamus' pack will take her in until we return." It was always their first safe house.

"Pack?" The sneer in Nico's tone made him look at her.

"Have an issue with shifters, because I can tell you, you're about to find you have an extended family of them."

"Filthy creatures."

"Just try not to say that around Seamus, he might take exception to you insulting his pups." She growled and bared her fangs, so he had a feeling there may be a battle before the war. "Momma, we have to take Lark to Seamus and then talk to Dominic. If Meadow and Tasha are hurt, they're at a human disadvantage."

"Lark, baby, let's go."

"You promise to bring her home, no matter what, you bring her home." Lark clutched at Amora t-shirt and made her mate meet her eyes.

"No matter what, I'll bring our baby home." No hesitation marked Amora's voice. She spoke with conviction. She would bring Meadow back.

The no matter what made him sick. The thought of Meadow and Tasha not surviving, as much as he wanted to ignore it, the possibility was there. It wasn't an option.

Amora darted a look at him over her mate's head and their eyes locked. A silent promise made, a vow that their family would be together once again and he nodded. He watched Amora lead Lark away to the bedroom to gather up an overnight bag and to give them a few minutes of privacy.

"Must be nice."

The wistfulness in Nico's tone confused him, and he turned to find her watching the space between two screens Amora and Lark disappeared through. He hadn't thought beyond what little he knew of Nico's life before the usual fucked Jackyl curse struck them again.

"What do you mean?"

"Nothing, I've always been alone, must be nice to love and be loved."

Before he could question her further, she walked away, pretending to explore the bookshelves, but he couldn't miss the sadness and lost look in her eyes. There was more to her story than what the scars told, but how much more?

* * *

A BATTLE HAD WAGED between them, and Seamus insisted on accompanying them. "Seamus, the fewer people in our party, the better. Keeping together so we can dematerialize if things go nuclear is going to be hard enough with just the three of us."

"I don't like it, but we can handle it. This mission won't be the first time we've done this. Vampires aren't invincible. You know weres are the superior species." Seamus folded his arms across his broad, barrel chest.

Nico snorted from behind him, and Ripper darted a warning glance at her. She held up her hands and wandered off to stand with her back to a corner. He didn't know what her issue with shifters was, but he didn't have time to play referee. Amora and Seamus were already squaring off for another epic battle. Not that a fight between the two wasn't entertaining, they just didn't have time for it right now.

"Superior, keep your mangy ass here. Like Ripper said, the smaller the team, the better right now. Stay on alert and keep my wife safe. Please, Seamus, if it comes down to it when we have to go after Tasha and Meadow, we'll come back."

Seamus appeared unconvinced, but eventually, they talked their way out of having pack members joining them, that included the Alpha. The conversation with Dominic would be contentious enough. Ripper laced his fingers with Amora and Nico, closed his eyes and imagined the old demon. Nico stumbled beside him as they appeared outside Dominic's chamber door.

Throwing back the tapestry, the deceptively bright smile on the demon's face didn't fool him.

"Ah, I am becoming quite popular, I see. Nicolette Medina-Jackyl, it is a pleasure, I have always been fascinated with your penchant for cruelty. So much blood on those hands, a warrior after my own blackened heart and I must admit the Medina-Jackyl's have always been such amusement. You all kill so effortlessly and relish it. Wear the blood of your enemies as a badge of honor and warning to others."

"Stuff it, old man." Nico stalked the edges of the chamber and Ripper watched her carefully. Every line of her body tensed and the fingers on her left hand flexed.

"What do I owe, Ripper, to see you so soon after our last lovely meeting?"

"Another fucking secret," Amora hissed beside him.

"Not the time, we'll shed blood over this after we complete the mission."

"Fine and don't think I'll forget it either."

Ripper grunted as Amora's fist connected with his abdomen. Dammit, she needed to tone down her violent tendencies.

"This touching moment of maternal love overwhelms me."

"Dominic, you know exactly why we're here?"

"Must you rob me of the little amusement that I have? Fine." Dominic let out a long-suffering sigh and gathered his robe around him as he sat in his chair in front of the fire. "You're missing something very precious, are you?"

"Amora." Ripper's voice held an edge of forewarning as he noticed his mother moving toward the demon. She growled as she leaned her shoulder against the stone wall and watched Dominic diligently. "Knock off the games...you know where my mate and Meadow are."

"It's possible that I'm in possession of such knowledge, was it not discussed that Meadow informed you not to come for her if they captured her?"

"Ripper, what the hell is he talking about? I'm getting tired of your secrets, boy."

He was going to answer, but Dominic spoke up first. "Our dear Meadow is a rather valuable instrument for Kali, but as much as he could use her skills as a Seer, there is something else that Meadow is in possession of, the Jackyl family love."

"Kali expected us to come for her; it's a trap." Nico piped up from her post near the exit.

The bastard just smirked as he drummed his long, claw-tipped fingers on the arms of his chair.

"But, there's more than that."

"Ah, yes, the one development he did not anticipate, the power of a child unborn."

Ripper stiffened but tried to hide his reaction.

"She is most powerful, especially for being part human, but she grows weak. The field she's protecting her mother with won't last long, nor will she if she continues."

"Are you telling me—" Dominic raised a skeletal hand to cut him off.

"I am telling you that your child is dying, the human side has made her weak. When she senses her mother in danger she reacts, it is rather interesting. I would love to study her if she survives."

It was too much, so he surged forward as the familiar tickle beneath his skin signaled the change. Fabric ripped as his body elongated, the bitter venom burst upon his tongue, and the warning shake of his rattle echoed off the walls.

An odd buzzing filled his head, and he didn't remember how his hands came to fist in the demon's robe or how the falsely frail body slammed back against the wall. Ripper's vision was red as murderous rage burned through his cold-blooded veins.

"Impressive. Even Kali isn't as deadly in his pure form."

The awe in Dominic's voice caused his eyes to narrow. He sensed Amora and Nico closed in yet still held back.

"Where are they?" A slow, slurring hiss infused his voice as his tongue slithered from between his thinned lips. "I will kill you in the most gruesome ways possible, but not before I make you beg for it. Talk!" The order boomed and shook the walls of the chamber.

"Open your troubled, rage-filled mind, Collector, I know not where they are, but you can feel your child. Even in the warm, safety of her mother's womb, she cries out to you."

Ripper hissed as his body coiled tightly and with a lazy flick of his wrists he sent Dominic soaring across the room. Mortar crumbled as the frail body fell to the floor.

"Ripper, stand down."

Amora's command barely registered as he pivoted on the soft scaled underbelly of his snake form. Weapon drawn she waited, Nico watched them warily, and he could see the dilemma in her gaze. Who to back up or battle them both? The indecision was evident, but he turned his narrowed eyes from them to focus back on the demon.

"You must control your beast, Jackyl, or the war is lost before the battle has begun. Meadow may have been the objective of Kali's latest folly, but Tasha is also as important. A grandchild to shape into the beast that he was unable to nurture in Demonus or you. She already possesses unbelievable power. Predisposed to limitless violence."

Ripper stalked Dominic's every move as the male pushed to his feet and dusted off his robe.

"Unfortunately, once again in his arrogance, he has overestimated his power. She's rather fearsome already, one capable of great love and cruelty. She is a fascinating creature already, not yet born, yet already so very loyal."

Ripper spun away as he dropped his eyes to the cobblestone floor and tried to clear his head. The demon's loyalty was questionable, but even in his cryptic information, there was always the truth.

Dominic despised Kali. The hate alighted in his eyes with each mention of the Soul Collector's name. Imprisonment destroyed whatever allegiance the ancient demon may have once possessed, and it would work in their favor.

Just focus, he closed his eyes to picture his mate. Tasha's smiling face, the happiness tinged with insecurity as she had pressed his hand to her belly. Her skin was silky beneath his lips as he brushed them to the subtle curve and smiled up at her. Ripper had wished so long for her, and he wouldn't lose her again, not now.

He pushed the presence of Dominic away, along with Nico and Amora, and fixated on Tasha and the presence of their daughter. The annoying buzz in his head turned to a calming hum. Contentment, Tasha lost in dreams, and their child was calm, yet alert. It was strange. He shook it off and concentrated entirely on them. Sadness flowed over him as he felt his child's heartbeat slowing.

Ripper surged across the room, his hands roughly gripped Nico and Amora's wrists. They protested, and he ignored them, they weren't there. Close by, another safe house, the air shifted and crackled around them as they disappeared leaving the old demon behind.

CHAPTER 20

Shivering, she hadn't thought the temperature could drop further—she was wrong, and she held Meadow tighter to her chest. The little girl drifted in and out of consciousness, her worry built to heart-stopping levels. Tasha couldn't let anything happen to Meadow. No one returned to check on them, and she sporadically slept. Time passed in agonizing increments, doubt flooded her with thoughts of them never finding them.

She removed the sling, wincing at the twinge and was thankful for the darkness that hid the damage. Tucking Ripper's shirt around them and added another layer to keep Meadow protected from the cold and Tasha's quickly chilling body wasn't helping.

"They're at the gate!"

Those four simple words descended everything outside their cell into chaos. Great booming reverberations of gunshots cracked the air. She swore she could feel each one. Screams of torment and bellows of rage rang out from everywhere, and her heart leaped in her chest. An explosion vibrated the walls of their cell.

"Tasha?" The weak utterance of her name pulled her attention to Meadow.

She gently squeezed Meadow and tried to sound optimistic. "You hear that? Ripper and Amora came for us."

"No!" The scream Meadow let out froze the blood in her veins. "Gonna die!" Tears dampened Tasha's chest as Meadow sobbed and uncontrollably shuddered in her arms.

"Tasha! Meadow!" Amora's voice rose above the battle sounds and the shrieks. Tasha struggled to her feet, holding Meadow one-armed as she weakly weaved toward the door.

"In here." Tasha's arm was useless so she could bang on the door to alert Amora of their whereabouts and could only hope the vamp could hear them. "Amora!"

"Stand back."

Tasha darted to the side seconds before the door exploded on its hinges. Amora stepped into the room, her eyes black and every line of her body rigid. Relief stole through the vampire's gaze.

"Give her to me," Amora demanded.

"I need help."

A fierce growl sounded deep in Amora's chest as the vamp's eyes fell on Tasha's useless arm. With quick, efficient movements she removed the child from beneath Tasha's shirt.

"Stay behind me, Nico and Ripper are up top, but they can only hold them off so long. When I say hide, you hide, do you understand?"

She nodded in answer and followed behind Amora. The grunts and bellows grew louder as they reached a staircase. Her foot caught on the step, and Amora grabbed her as she started to fall. Tasha felt as useless as her arm.

Cresting the top of the stairs, Amora darted a look left and right, then left again. Grit abraded the bottoms of Tasha's bare feet as the hallway opened into a cavernous room.

"Take her."

Tasha grabbed Meadow as Amora tucked them into a corner.

"Whatever you do don't scream, don't draw attention." It was impossible to answer around the lump in her throat.

Ripper's demon form caught her eye, seemingly larger and more dangerous than the one other time she'd seen him. Nausea burned and twisted her gut as lethal, black claws tore into defenseless human flesh. Blood splashed across his shiny onyx skin.

Arms, legs, and heads severed as they kept coming at him. He hissed, and she bit her lip to keep from crying out as she watched the beautiful midnight skin split beneath the slicing of blades.

"Amora!"

A strange, female voice drew her attention away from Ripper. A spinning kick from the lean woman caused an enraged roar from the woman's attacker. In the minute it took to blink, a blade sliced through the air embedding into the side of the male's throat. He clawed at the knife and ripped it out sending a gushing of dark red through the air. His legs failed him, and he dropped to his knees with a death gurgle.

She hid Meadow's face against her chest, but she couldn't pull her eyes away from the scene in front of her. Amora and the female worked in perfect harmony, backs pressed together. Their every movement synchronized, pivoting and kicking as they took on assailants from all sides. Each woman wore twin smiles, feral and frightening. Tasha could almost hear the hard-edged laughter.

The creature her boss truly was never occurred to her until now, protective and loyal, but the extent of the danger astounded her. Another roar caused her to flinch as her eyes darted back to Ripper. Ripper's body was tightly coiled around a large male, and the man's face was purple as his eyes bugged from their sockets. Her mate ignored the male as he fought a steady line of men. A solid phalanx three rows deep.

His head fell back on his shoulders as the reverberation of gunshots broke the tense concentration of the battle. Tasha covered her mouth to silence or at least muffle her scream as shots peppered Ripper's back. Ripper's body jerked with each shot that connected. He turned, the strength of his lower body swept the men off their feet as he faced the coward who shot him in the back.

He was nothing but a surge of rippling muscle as he moved with fluid grace across the cold stone floor and the male's eyes widened, his mouth fell slack in a soundless scream. Ripper's strong hands dripped with blood as they circled the shooter's throat. Tasha swallowed back the bile that burned bitterly at the sound of bone cracking as Ripper twisted and broke his neck.

She couldn't watch any longer, she dropped her gaze to Meadow and hid her face against the child's thin shoulder. Meadow spoke not a word, she seemed lost in some other place, and her gaze was a vacant stare. No reaction to the death happening around them, Tasha knew this carnage wouldn't end until Ripper, Amora and the other woman —she assumed was Nicolette—were the only ones still standing.

As before time dragged by, yet instead of silence, time was measured in screams, grunts, and bloodshed. Death surrounded them, how had she come to this moment? Was this what life as a Medina-Jackyl would be, would she worry about Ripper every time he left her to pursue vendettas centuries old? A sense of dread overtook her, would she forever be terrified of losing him?

No, her mind screamed for her to push away the thoughts and endless questions. This was her family, her mate protecting her and the depths of their loyalty shocked her. They had put their lives, centuries of existence on the line to save her and Meadow. Her biological family wouldn't go that far. Somewhere at a distance, she heard everything go silent, and she lifted her head.

Bodies piled up in a macabre display, a floor bathed in blood and Ripper towered over it all. His deep green eyes found her, lowering his upper body to the ground he made his way toward her. His blood-drenched hands reached for her, yet hesitated. Tasha could see the indecision and pain in his gaze. She knew what he thought, she reached out with her good hand and wrapped her arm around the back of his neck.

He gathered them both against his chest, his strong embrace held them comfortably. Amora came forward, silently removed Meadow from between them. Tasha held desperately to him, buried her face in the coolness of his throat as she let the tears she'd held in stream down her cheeks. She didn't care about the blood or the unknown chunks she didn't want to know the origins.

Adrenaline receded under the surge of relief, and her arm began to throb.

"We have to go...more are coming."

The stranger's voice broke the spell and Ripper gathered them all in his arms. The strange tingling traveled over her skin as the world shifted.

"Amora, Meadow!" Lark's voice called out, and Tasha lifted her head, they were in the center of a circle of colorful caravans.

"Ripper, I have a Healer to see to your mate." A gruff male voice caused her eyes to lift way up.

"Seamus, thank you."

She felt Ripper's body return to normal as he swept her into his lean, powerful arms. He ignored his nudity and for some reason she cast her gaze around, keen female eyes watched him. Tasha didn't realize she'd rumbled until she heard Ripper's chuckle.

"Easy, baby, you're not battle ready just yet."

They entered the shade of a large tent, the smoky scent of incense permeated the space, and she sighed as he lowered her into a soft nest of pillows and blankets.

"I'll send someone with water for you to clean up and fresh clothes, then Morgana will be here shortly to attend your mate."

Tasha watched the two men embrace one-armed, and Ripper lowered his head in respect. She was confused by the interaction; it was that of a father and son. "I'll leave you to your mate."

"Thank you again."

"Ripper, no matter what, as with Amora, you'll always be a member of my pack. We take care of our own."

A nod was Ripper's only answer before her mate fell to his knees beside her.

"Are you okay? Is the baby?" The words broke with barely held sobs as his hands moved over every inch of her, but lingered on the new curve of her belly. Before now she hadn't paid much attention to the new roundness. Were Demon/Vamp babies quicker to form and mature?

"Oh." She watched tears brighten Ripper's eyes as his hands tenderly stroked and he pushed her shirt up. She was speechless at the raw emotion in his bright jade eyes.

His head lowered until his mouth brushed her stomach. "Sleep, you did so good."

"What's wrong? Is the baby okay?" Panic caused her voice to come out a few octaves higher, and the words squeaked as she brought her good hand to her stomach. What if the baby wasn't okay? What if she'd failed to protect him or her?

"I tried, they stomped, but I curled into a ball, I swear I tried, Ripper, I promise I did." The flow of her words ceased as lips slammed to hers, a kiss flavored with the salt of their tears.

"She's fine." Ripper pulled back, yet didn't separate their mouths.

"She?"

"We have a beautiful and healthy little girl in there." He cupped the sides of her stomach.

She had more questions to ask, but a beautiful woman with long, silver hair plaited into a thick braid over her shoulder breezed into the tent.

"Ripper, get cleaned up, I'll check your wounds after I check on your mate and child." A friendly smile made the woman glow as she set down a quilted bag and lowered to her knees. "You must be Tasha. I'm Morgana...I'm the pack's healer. May I?" Hands hovered over her stomach, and she nodded. "Magnificent."

Ripper kissed her quickly, and as he stood, a scruffy man entered the tent. "Seamus sent clothes and water." Her mate took the large brass bucket and the stack of neatly folded clothes.

"He's not going anywhere, dear." Warmth infused the woman's hands as they stroked gently over her stomach. "A powerful child, you are very blessed."

"Is she really okay?"

"Absolutely perfect, a bit tired from expending too much energy."

"What do you mean?"

"She protected you." Morgana closed her eyes and sighed. "Erected a field of energy. Most unusual for an unborn child, but it did work in your favor."

"Is she, will she…" Tasha didn't know how to ask, and the words wouldn't come.

"Her demon and vampire sides are much stronger than her human part, which is normal. A new species of sorts, rather remarkable, and as a defense mechanism, she accelerated her growth. Your daughter is sleeping soundly and is perfectly healthy. Will you allow me to heal your arm?"

Tasha only nodded as she tried to pull her thoughts together. Relief took over knowing her child was safe, but what about Meadow? "Is Meadow okay?"

"She will be, there is much to learn about that one. Meadow is lost, pulled deeply into herself, but she's healthy, and I healed her wounds as well."

Tasha flinched as soft hands circled her forearm, she cried out as pain tore through her. Suddenly the woman was knocked a few feet backward.

"I'm sorry, I should have been more careful." Morgana pressed her face close to Tasha's stomach, gently whispered words and once more took Tasha's arm.

The pain eased as she watched the softly glowing hands and then darted wide eyes at Morgana. "What…" Morgana hushed her. She watched as a dark bruise formed on Morgana's arm, and she gasped.

"I am quite accustomed to the pain, Tasha, please don't fret."

Tasha couldn't take her eyes from Morgana as the woman deftly lifted to her feet.

"Ripper, I'll return later to check in again on Tasha. Now, let me attend to your wounds."

Tasha observed Ripper as he rolled his eyes and shook his head.

"Yes, I'm quite certain you're capable of healing naturally, but humor this old woman."

"You are not old, Morgana."

Tasha watched through a haze of confusion as she tried to process all that happened. The world was so much different than she had grown up to believe. Would she ever understand? Her lashes fluttered along her cheekbones as exhaustion pulled her down. Fighting it was useless, she curved her hands around her stomach and let sleep take her. There would be time enough later for all the questions she needed answered.

CHAPTER 21

*R*ipper crossed his arms over his chest and watched Tasha sleep; then he glanced over his shoulder as he sensed his mother enter the tent. "How's Meadow?"

"Something's not right. She's catatonic, Morgana says she's healthy. The head wound healed perfectly. What about Tasha and the baby?" Amora and Ripper stood shoulder to shoulder, both of them tensed as was usual for them when they were on alert.

"Both are fine. I sent for Demonus." He didn't know if it would do any good to have his father there, but they needed as many heads in the game as they could get.

"Why?"

Ripper almost grunted a chuckle at her open disgust. His parents were best friends—even if they liked to deny it—but Amora hated when Demonus was brought into the family business. It sometimes amused him how his mother considered his father inferior for his overabundance of testosterone.

"I hope he has answers for us. The fact we were allowed to escape a little too easily makes me apprehensive."

"You call what happened easy?"

The disbelief in his mother's tone made him smile sadly.

"Yeah, Angelus would know that I'd destroy that small army he left if I brought along my badass warrior mom." His attempt at a joke fell flat. "The fucker is up to something, which is nothing new, but I have to know what it is. I have to keep them safe. I already failed them."

Strong fingers gripped the back of his neck and forced his eyes to Amora's—anger flared in her gaze.

"You failed no one, your mate and child are alive. Don't borrow trouble, don't bring guilt onto yourself where it isn't deserved."

He knew Amora was right that he couldn't anticipate Kali taking Tasha and Meadow. Knowing she was right and accepting it was two different issues.

Energy crackled the air as Demonus appeared, his usually neat blond hair stood up as if he had repeatedly run his fingers through it.

"Why wasn't I notified before you marched the Jackyl Death Squad into battle?"

"Hello to you too, Demonus. So lovely to see you again."

"Don't mess with me, Amora, I'm not in the mood for your invincible Alpha Vamp Female bullshit. Males are not second-class citizens."

"Tone down the bitching. Damn, you gotta be quicker, Kali, you were always late."

"Fuck you, Amora. How's Tasha and the baby? Is our grandchild okay?"

Ripper stepped in before it de-escalated into a total pissing contest —they loved the who's strap-on/cock was bigger game. Who needed normal friends? Normal parents would've been nice. "She's fine, Dad, Morgana took care of them. I want to know what the fuck Angelus is up too."

"That old bastard has lost his mind." Demonus shoved his hands through his hair again. "Or whatever he had left of one, he's completely locked down the compound. I'm barred from entering his realm."

"Hiding away with his ass tucked between his legs," Amora growled.

"I need to see Meadow."

Demonus' voice dropped to a deep growl and Ripper darted a look at his dad. The demon visibly rippled beneath the male's skin. There was one thing his Dad never let out, and that was his demon, rarely did the male even shift for pleasure.

They exited the tent with no further discussion and Ripper called over a guard to take a post at the tent's opening. Sunrise was quickly approaching, so only a few sentries and vampires roamed the camp. They approached Amora's caravan. Ripper and Amora stopped at the doorway. Demonus entered, and Lark came instantly awake.

His father crouched beside the bunk and reached out, his hand pushed the curls back from Meadow's face. Her eyes stared forward, and she hadn't spoken a word since they'd arrived.

A look of concern transformed the angles of Demonus' face causing them to soften.

"She warned me that the bad man would take her, he said that Amora and I'd come for her. Meadow told me not to. I took her to Selena."

"What did the witch have to say?"

"That she's a Foreteller of Death. I guess she's an Untouchable like Morgana. Dominic sort of confirmed what she said. I don't know how developed her skill is or if it's still dormant."

"Again, your secretive shit will be dealt with after we take care of Kali and his power trip."

"I look forward to it."

"She's trapped. A child of this age, with the power she possesses, who knows what she's seen. I fear she saw more than she was able to handle. Surrounded by the amount of death I'm sure you three caused, and by the way, Nicolette is not a healthy addition to the Jackyl level of extreme psychoses."

"Quit whining about not being asked to come out and play with us. Now, back to grown-up business."

"Are you saying she won't awaken?" As soon as Lark's voice broke with grief, Amora was at her mate's side.

"To be honest, Lark, I can't say. I fear what Angelus has done. From what I learned, he was grooming her for the position as a Seer. We're not safe here. Everyone we love and care for is in danger. Ripper?" He lifted his head and met his father's eyes. "You know what needs done, but I know you're not ready. You need to challenge Angelus for his throne."

"I'm not ready."

"Ready or not, Ripper, it's time to take your birthright by any means necessary. You may leave him alive, but it's time. Banish him to his realm."

"And if I don't survive? What happens to my mate, our child? Does she become the next to suffer under the weight of rule? I can't subject her to that fate. Our daughter doesn't deserve that."

"Then do what has to be done. If you can't accept, then leave him alive to rule, but make your position quite clear. Kali is weak, he doesn't possess the power he used to, and I have no doubt you can easily defeat him. It has to be done, Ripper. Are you ready to show Kali what a Medina-Jackyl is truly made of?"

Ripper placed his hands on his hips, dropping his chin to his chest. Demonus spoke the truth—he needed to challenge Kali. But was he ready to become what he'd fought so hard against? The problem was to figure out how to succeed without completely losing his mate and child.

"I need to speak with Tasha."

He didn't wait for a reply from his parents, he turned on his toes and headed back to the tent. Dismissing the guard, he bent slightly and entered. He resumed his position of watching over Tasha.

He'd never been a coward, well he had, but that was only when he believed Tasha would deny being his. Ripper was confident he could make Kali submit, banish him to his realm and take his birthright.

If it were only him, he wouldn't feel so conflicted, but he had Tasha and their daughter to consider. Would she accept him as the monster he was or turn him away to save herself? He feared finding out yet before he could make a decision, Tasha and he needed to discuss it.

"Ripper?"

He forced a smile at her quiet voice and closed the distance between them.

"What's wrong? Don't bullshit me. I can see it in your eyes."

"What happened while they held you? Did they take Meadow at any time?"

"No, they separated us when they took me, but when I returned to the cell, she was right where I left her. But..." He waited for her to continue, but she remained silent.

"What, what happened? It's important, Tasha. Something is wrong with Meadow."

"When she, when we heard the fight begin, I told her that y'all were there to save us. She screamed, terrified and she said we were all going to die. After that, Amora had arrived, and Meadow went silent. What's happening?"

"It seems that Meadow was to serve Angelus. I don't know what he did, but she's lost inside her head. Just stares off into space, her eyes are dead. Tasha..." He cleared his throat. "I have to make a decision, and I can't do that without you."

"Decision?" She looked away, and he watched as she stroked her stomach in small circles. He placed his hand over hers, his thumb stroking the upper curve.

"I have to challenge Kali. He's powerful, but I can take what is mine. I can leave him alive and possibly postpone my fate. He's drunk with power, he's becoming mad, and I've got to stop him now."

"Will we be safe?"

The sadness that flashed through his mate's gaze tore him up inside.

"If I can make him submit, banish him, he'll always be a danger to us. For you and her." He lay down, placed his head in Tasha's lap and rested his forehead on her stomach. "I have to try, I love you, and I promise, if necessary, I'll fight through Hell to come back to you."

Ripper closed his eyes as the silence lengthened. He didn't open them, not wanting to face the hurt he knew he'd see in her gaze. Soft fingers carded through his hair. "You do what you need for our family, I..." She stopped talking, and he opened his eyes, tears hung on her lower lashes. "Love you. I'll be here waiting."

He rolled to his hands and knees, loomed over her as his mouth found hers and he kissed her gently. Tasha's hands cupped his cheeks as she opened for him.

Silently he undressed her, exposed the lush curves of her form. He worshiped her with hands and lips, and soft whimpers turned to a cry as he moved into the cradle of her thighs. Their eyes locked as he slid into the warm, welcoming body. He loved her, making his promise in the slow, tender loving and the brush of his lips along her tear-stained cheeks.

* * *

RIPPER APPEARED ONCE MORE outside the gates of Kali's compound. The presence of guards had doubled since the last time. He reached behind his back, his fingertips popped the clasps that held the silver knives in place, and he closed his eyes as metal slithered slowly from leather with a low hiss. He dropped his arms to his sides, his eyes opened, and a savage sneer pulled at the corners of his mouth.

"Let the games begin."

His knees bent, and he pushed upward, his body soared over the fence. Before he touched the ground, he'd shifted and landed on his soft, ridged belly. Guards yelled for assistance, but their utterances turned to wet, gurgling gasps as he lashed out. Razor sharp tips split their throats in macabre gaping smiles. He moved in blurred motions as they all fell and he didn't stop until he felt the substantial barrier of the portal.

He shifted as he threw himself against the barrier, electric blue sparks crackled around him as it gave. Scents of animals, most likely feral shifters teeming with bloodlust, greeted him. He spun the blades upon his palms, gripped the hilts in his fists and placed them along his forearms. His belly slithered upon the ground while venom burned on his tongue as they converged. They arrived on all fours, and claws dug into the loose earth to gain purchase, then they reared onto hind legs. The bite of their claws a nuisance as he battled his way toward Kali's house.

Ripper's needle-sharp fangs deeply pierced feline and lupine flesh, immense, agonized cries as venom ate away at their insides. Dissolving muscle and flesh turned into quivering bloody masses of tangled, bloody pelts. Keening howls echoed in the distance as the others began to arrive, but stopped. They dropped their heads and backed away. The ones still alive rolled to their backs exposing their bellies in submission.

"Kali," he yelled. As he made his way to the house, the door opened, and Cecil stepped out, then to the side.

"Has the time come?"

Kali walked nude onto the porch, and as he moved slowly down the steps, his form shifted. The crack of breaking bones was loud as his body elongated. Where Ripper's flesh was the color of shimmering onyx with hints of green, Kali's was the deepest shade of emerald.

"Do you think you're ready, boy?"

Joints popped as Kali flexed his hands. Ripper threw his blades aside and they sunk deep into the ground. They circled each other as their eyes carefully took in each subtle movement. Looking for an opening and anticipating who would strike first.

"You've brought this upon yourself, Kali. You've attacked my family for the last time. Submit, agree to banishment and I won't have to force you."

The chilling laugh cut through the quiet just as Kali charged. Ripper spun to the side and used the bastard's momentum against him. His tail connected with Kali's stomach and he quickly coiled around the male. Claws pierced the deep ridges of his abdomen and raked upward, flesh split as blood flowed to the ground. The black acidic sludge sizzled upon the grass.

Kali spun, an elbow connected with Ripper's jaw and he recoiled.

"Ripper!"

He was distracted by the sound of Meadow's voice. The little girl barely made it out the front door before Cecil wrapped his arms around her. He restrained her from nearing the violence. He hissed as he met the old man's eyes and saw him nod.

He paid for the distraction as Kali slammed their bodies together and he hit the ground. Their forms curled around each other, claws and teeth ripped at flesh. Exchanging blows back and forth, he felt the fight dying from Kali as the male weakened. His grandfather fought with a ferocity borne of desperation. An old man at the end of his rope, no longer as invincible as he wanted to appear.

With a quick shift of his body, he overtook Kali and bore the male into the ground beneath him. "Give, and I'll allow you to live; keep fighting, and I'll kill you with no guilt."

"Fucking half-breed, a pathetic creature, nothing more than a sickly child. Your loyalty is misplaced—a whore and a bastard child."

He hissed as he reared back, with an arc of his arm he brought his claws across Kali's face. Kali's cheek split wide, and his tongue lolled out as Ripper lost control, strike upon strike, ripping away flesh, muscle, and bone. The lethal tip of his nail caught Kali's eye causing thick, viscous fluid to flow as the eyeball ruptured and oozed from the socket.

"Ripper!" He surged away, Kali lay upon the ground unmoving, and he slithered gracefully along the ground until he reached Meadow.

"Are you okay?" He kept his distance to keep his blood off her delicate skin. He didn't want to chance that what happened to her in this realm wouldn't afflict her back home.

"I want to go home, but he won't let me. I want Momma." He wanted to embrace and comfort her. Instead, he lowered his head until his mouth was next to her ear.

"Close your eyes, picture your Momma, and Lark, Tasha. Forget about everything else, just imagine them." He lightly stroked her silky hair as she relaxed. She began to fade, and her soul returned to her body.

"Cecil, I'm not ready to ascend, when the bastard awakens tell him that if I have to return, I'll bring his whole, fucked up kingdom down without mercy. Better yet, tell him to hide and forget he ever heard the Medina-Jackyl name."

"You will ascend one day, Ripper. It was foretold long before your birth. Why postpone the inevitable? Why allow him more chances to strike out at you and your family?" He remained silent, but the shrewd old man smiled at him. "You can't figure a way out, Master Ripper. You cannot deny your destiny or that one day that future will belong to your heir as well."

"A few more years of normalcy or whatever normal I can have as a Jackyl, Cecil, just don't forget to deliver my message."

"As you wish, I'll be honored to serve you one day, but let's hope it's not too soon."

Ripper nodded as he cast one last glance at his grandfather's prone frame. Normalcy, a family with Tasha and life on their terms before he was no longer in control of his fate. He wasn't ready to be a puppet to some prophecy. He refused, but he hoped leaving the bastard in existence wouldn't come back to haunt him and his family.

CHAPTER 22

*T*asha wiped tears from her eyes as Meadow awakened with a gasp. Lark and Amora crushed the little girl between them. Demonus stepped to the side and came to stand beside her. He slipped an arm around her, and she relaxed into his side.

"One less soul for Angelus to possess and that's an excellent sign that your mate will be home soon."

"How do you know?"

"Have some faith, Tasha. That son of mine will do everything he can to come home to you and—" Demonus pressed his hand to her stomach, and her eyes shot to his face. "She will be so much like him, strong and loyal, and a fierce warrior that will rival Amora."

"Am I going to have to worry about her like I do him?"

Tasha was on the edge of losing her calm. How was she going to live if Ripper didn't come home to her?

"She's a Jackyl, and like a Jackyl, she's a fighter from conception. My granddaughter is a hellion. I can already feel it."

"You don't have to look so happy about it."

"Oh, I'm well aware of how Ripper was before and after birth. She'll be a beautiful creature, irresistible. Amora and I have already discussed where to dispose of the bodies of would-be suitors."

She knew what he was doing, and she appreciated his attempt to take her mind off the uncertainty of her mate's future.

"Lark has already offered to hide bodies. I'm wondering if I even want to belong to this bloodthirsty family." She knew it was a joke, Tasha wanted to a part of the Jackyl's. Revenge, and with them, she'd always felt at home. Comforted and loved, she wouldn't give that up, but she still needed time to process it all.

"Yes, you do. We're in possession of questionable morals, but family is everything and if we can't hide a few pesky bodies, what's the point?" Tasha bumped Demonus with her shoulder as he chuckled and tightened his embrace.

"Is he alive?"

"Yes." He spoke with conviction, but she wondered if he was only attempting to soothe her nerves.

Tasha wanted to believe him—needed to in fact. Any other option would break her heart, to come so close to having what she'd always wanted and lose it all was too cruel to contemplate.

"Thank you."

"You are my son's mate, my daughter-in-law and the mother of my grandchild. Your gratitude is unnecessary. I'm happy and proud my son found you. You both deserve all the happiness you two can find together. Now, would you like me to walk you back to your tent?"

As she was about to answer, a breeze stirred in the arrival of night. She spun on her toes just as the familiar form of her mate appeared in the middle of camp. Gripping the sides of her skirt, she took off running toward him. Uncaring of the blood encrusted body, heedless of his wounds, she threw herself into his arms. His embrace drove the breath from her lungs as she held him. Tears of relief and happiness streamed down her cheeks as he spun her off her feet.

His hold grew weak as his body seemed to sag. Ripper's eyes closed and she called his name. She wrapped him in her arms.

"Demonus, Amora!"

When her gaze searched Ripper, she took in the deep lacerations to his chest, and her stomach became sick as she saw the exposed muscle and bone.

"Morgana." Amora's voice called for the healer and Tasha fought against the strong arms that tried to pull her away.

Her boss bent over Ripper's body. Amora took her son's cheeks in her hands and called his name. Ripper was lost in the limbo of shifting, somewhere between demon and human form.

"Tasha, calm yourself. Tasha!"

She pulled her eyes away from her fallen mate and turned on Demonus, ready to fight to get back to Ripper.

"Pull it together. You stand tall and strong for Ripper. It's your job as a mate." His voice held an edge of command that belied the concern on his face.

Strong, she could do that, for Ripper and she took a deep breath, then released it slowly. She turned back to Ripper as Seamus and Morgana arrived. As the Alpha scooped Ripper into his arms, muscles bulged under the strain of Ripper's weight.

Thoughts of losing Ripper had only been abstract nightmares, but now it was all too real. Demonus slipped his arm around her waist as he guided her back to the tent they'd given her. Her steps faltered outside the entry.

"Don't mourn before his time, Tasha."

She nodded at the warning and ducked through the opening. It was chaos inside. Seamus and Amora quickly washed the blood from their arms and hands. Skin smoked where thick blood the color of midnight ate away the fabric first and then the skin beneath.

Morgana placed her hands on the open wounds, but the pain must have been too great. She lifted the sides of her skirt and hurried to her mate.

"He's too badly injured to heal on his own. His blood is like acid." Frustration tinged Morgana's voice as she tried again. Tasha's stomach recoiled at the scent of burning flesh.

"Do you have to touch him directly?"

Morgana turned confused gray eyes on her and Tasha laid her hands over the wound that was nothing more than flesh cleaved back. She closed her eyes and bit the inside of her lips.

"It's best to touch, but we'll see."

Gentle, yet strong hands rested on hers, and she felt the tingling heat that she remembered from the Healer tending Tasha's arm. The skin seemed to stitch together slowly beneath her hands. Time dragged out, endlessly as they moved from one injury to the next, until the last deep laceration sealed into thick scar tissue.

"Why isn't he…" Her voice broke, and the weakness shamed her.

"Tasha, he needs to feed."

There was no mistaking what Amora meant as the vamp spoke from behind her.

"Have you—"

She jerked her head from side to side. He'd always heated blood up and drank it. Ripper had never asked her.

"Demonus, take Morgana and tend her hands, send in warm water to bathe Ripper."

Tasha realized Amora had dismissed everyone from the tent.

"What do I do?"

"With the pregnancy, we just kinda thought you'd already tapped a vein for him."

"He never asked it of me. Didn't I give him…" Soft lips touched the damp fringe of her lashes.

"No doubts, darlin'. With you being mortal and all, we'll be careful, especially with my grandspawn in residence."

Amora had shifted seconds before Tasha heard the whisper of steel from the sheath at the small of Amora's back. A cold, steady hand took hers, rested it palm up, and she breathed deep and slow as the deadly sharp edge pressed to her palm. She flinched at the sting as skin separated under the slight pressure.

"Why didn't it ever occur to me? Some part of me thought he was invincible. I was stupid."

She went through the motions and Amora placed her hand over Ripper's lips. A memory of the gentleness of his kisses, his touch and the loving way he treated her. Regret for all the time she'd wasted pushing him away made the tears flow quicker down her cheeks. Her teeth sank into her lower lips to stifle the sobs.

"I said no doubts, Tasha. Knowing about us isn't the same as understanding. You look at the demon he is, the resilient image of what he is beneath the human frailty. I'm sorry. Explaining shit like this, we never know how to get it all out. I'm sure Lark doesn't know all the details."

"I should have known. I'm—" She flinched as Ripper's tongue stroked over the cut on her palm and the sting of the pull as he fed.

The pallor of his skin changed from chalky white to the natural healthy tan with a shimmer of the snake rippling beneath. Tasha felt as if she'd failed him in some way. Her free hand stroked the soft, golden hair streaked with blood back from his forehead. Strong fingers curled around her hand and held it to his mouth.

"Easy, Ripper. Take it slow." The pressure eased at the gentle murmur of Amora's voice.

Leaning down, Tasha pressed her lips to Ripper's ear. "You have to get better for me. I can't—" A sob cut off what she was going to say, and she shuddered as a strong arm twined around her waist pulling her down next to him. She ignored the blood and quickly mending wounds as she curled her body around him.

Nearly losing him broke her heart. Tasha took for granted the possibility that he could die. Their daughter came close to never knowing him.

"Baby, don't." His breath ruffled her hair.

"I can't help it." Long, slender fingers curled around the swell of her stomach as he dropped kisses all over her face.

"We're fine, you, me and our daughter. Nothing happened. I came back. I promised you I would."

Tasha lifted her tear-stained face, and her blurry gaze met the clear green of his eyes.

The lump in her throat threatened to choke her and made speaking impossible. She sensed when Amora left them alone. All the changes seemed ridiculous, going from denying herself the one man she never thought she'd have to being his mate, the mother of his child. It was too much to get her mind around, and she laid her head on his chest, let the gravelly rumble of his voice soothe her as she waited for what disaster came next.

CHAPTER 23

*R*ipper sat at the bar of Club Revenge, he nursed his drink and darted glances over his shoulder, trying to catch glimpses of Tasha. Since they returned from Seamus' camp, Tasha seemed to be pulling away. This was where they were supposed to be planning their future. Instead, Ripper felt like he was losing his mate. Some part of him had felt this coming; she would find being with him too much trouble. She slept in his arms each night, but that's as close as she'd let him.

Waiting for her to tell him they were over was killing him. Amora only said to give her time. Why should he have to put off the inevitable? Her rejection whether today or months from now would cause the same pain, losing her and their child was ripping his heart apart.

Last call quickly approached, with it would come stony silence and holding her stiff body in his embrace. Tasha wouldn't relax until she slipped to sleep. He'd made the decision to confront her the night before as he listened to the weeping she tried to hide from him. Her scent pulled his attention to the corridor that led to the dressing room and office.

His mother's gaze burned into his flesh and he shot her a glare, silently warning her to leave it alone.

"I don't give a fuck about your death glares, Rache. This bullshit has to stop. You two are too fucking stubborn for your own goods. I'd prefer if my grandspawn arrived in a happy home." Amora's fists clenched on the bar surface. "Don't think I haven't heard her crying herself to sleep for more than a week. Fix this. I won't allow my family to be torn apart."

"This isn't your concern, Ma."

"I am the matriarch of this family. Everything that's going on is my concern."

Ripper pushed his glass across the bar top, turned and stood. Tasha's gaze widened as she watched him approach. Indecision darkened her eyes, stay or flee, the question clear as she attempted to look away and hide what he could read there.

"Ripper, I have things I need—" Her excuses ceased as he trapped her with an arm around her waist and walked her backward.

Once in the dimly lit hallway, he closed his eyes to picture the house that they were to share and make a home. He ignored the fisting of her fingers in his t-shirt as the air around them changed, shifted, and when next he opened his eyes, they stood in the empty living room.

He released her as she stepped back, putting distance between them. It was the only consolation he would allow because this couldn't continue.

"Tasha, you have a decision to make. I don't want some bullshit runaround. Do you want to be with me? I can't take this—" His agitated motions indicated the space that separated their bodies. "—space and tension, I can't guarantee normal, and one day I won't have a choice."

He blew out a heavy breath as he watched her chin lower to her chest, but not before he noticed the shimmer of tears upon her lashes. "I almost lost you. I should have known—" Tasha's voice broke.

"What should you have known, baby?" Taking a step toward her and froze when she moved away.

"Amora had to tell me you needed to feed; why didn't I know?"

"Oh, baby." His hands shot out and grabbed her upper arms before she could move farther away. "I didn't, we hadn't talked about that, and I'm sorry, there's still so much."

Why hadn't he thought about that, the few times he had bitten her was during sex. He'd existed on donor blood most of his existence, Ripper didn't feed like other vamps and wasn't required to. "I don't feed like Amora. I require it, but not in large doses. I hunt in my demon form."

"Angelus' attack, you almost dying, I felt so helpless and stupid when Amora had to tell me what to do. She assumed because of the baby that I was already feeding you."

Ripper pulled back and took her face in his hands, stroked his thumbs along the damp, fringe of her lashes.

"Tasha." He kissed her tear-dampened lips, tasted the salt of her sadness. "I'm so sorry. I'm new at all this relationship stuff. Before you, I never wanted one. Amora and I, we've lived with this for so long, were surrounded by people, whether human or not, that understood. I love you, have loved you since the moment I met you. You were destined for me."

"Why me? You could have anyone, especially someone that knew how—" Ripper cut her off with a rough kiss and then pressed his forehead to hers to look deep into her eyes.

"You are everything I have ever wanted!" Desperation filled his chest. He needed her to understand. "You are perfect, every curve and nothing will ever change the way I feel about you. Why would you think I would settle for anyone that isn't you?"

Trembling hands rested on his cheeks. "I'm not strong enough, Ripper. I don't know if I can be what—" He growled against her lips and attempted to keep his anger in check.

"Stop, Tasha, please. I looked for you for almost a century, and there is no way I am going to give you up. You love me, I love you and our daughter, we can get through this. Please, baby, don't ask me to let you go. I'm not strong enough for that." He pled with her, and he would beg her to give him the chance to prove they were meant for each other.

Her tears were bitter agony on his tongue as he repeatedly pressed kisses to her lips. Whispering his love against the quivering lush curves of her mouth, Ripper had to make her understand. Part of him would die without her. He'd never felt this helpless. To have her turn away, deny what they were to each other broke his heart, the pain in his chest was excruciating. He would take any amount of torture, bear anything to have her accept him, demon and all.

"You accepted my demon, let the monster love you and I can't, dammit, Tasha, I refuse to let you go. Tell me you love me, tell me we can work through this. You're my mate, my heart, the reason I fought Angelus to come back to you. Please, baby, tell me," he demanded in husky, pain-filled tones and ignored the emotion that cracked his pleas.

"I love you."

Those were the only words he needed, his mouth crushed down on hers as his arms circled her and lifted her high on his chest. His tongue stroked hers, and he growled into her mouth as her legs twined around his waist. Tasha's nails stroked along his cheeks; their breaths were harsh. He walked through the house, toward the staircase and carried her up. His boots rang loudly through the empty house as he reached the top landing and made his way toward the master bedroom.

Nudging the door open with the toe of his boot, he strode toward the massive bed in the middle of the room. He laid her back on the bed he'd bought for them. The crisp cotton of the comforter touched his forearms as the mattress dipped beneath their weight.

Ripper broke the kiss, resting his weight on his knees as not to press on the curve of her stomach. Her fingertips stroked over his forearms as he shifted his body and moved lower. He pushed the shirt up over her stomach, her skin warm against his mouth.

"Ripper?" His name a mere breath of sound as she combed her fingers through his hair.

"Thank you for her, Tasha," he whispered and closed his eyes. This was a dream he'd always denied he wanted or needed. Ripper had pushed away all thoughts of a family, a mate, and a child.

"Do you know I refused to believe I wanted this? Growing up, I tried to be like Amora. The killing was easy, the bounty jobs, I followed in her footsteps, but something was always missing."

"What did you think that was?"

He sighed as she scraped her nails through his hair and over his scalp. "I swore I was content with it being only Amora and me, not allowing myself even to wish for this." Stroking his fingertips over the subtle curves, he cupped the sides of her small belly. A barely discernable flutter pushed against his right palm and his chest swelled with love, pride.

"I hadn't either. I distanced myself from my family years ago, and as I grew older—" She paused, and he heard the ragged inhalation. "What happens now?"

"We get our house ready, have my Bitch Mother marry us." He grinned as she chuckled.

"Are you going to find the others, like you did Nico?"

A hint of fear existed in the question. He couldn't lie, Angelus remained a threat, and they needed definitive answers on the rest of the siblings.

"If Nico survived, there's a chance the rest did as well. Naomi died, but what about Bram or the baby? If there's even a chance, I have to try. The last few months have brought up more questions than answers."

"I know, I understand, but I'm terrified." If not for his acute hearing he wouldn't have heard her speak.

"You have to trust me, Tasha. I have you and our daughter to come home too. It—" Ripper paused. "I won't be alone. Amora and Nico, family fights for their own." Shaking hands gripped his hair and pulled him up her body, her mouth pressed against his with silent promises.

Danger encircled the Medina-Jackyl family, centuries of death existing within shadows and demons breathing down their necks. The only way they could be safe was to destroy Angelus, to find the siblings and pull in ranks. They would finish it, their questions would finally have answers, but for tonight, his mate was in his arms.

His world was as it should be. Losing himself in the sweetness of Tasha's kiss, exposing the warmth of her curves and sliding perfectly into her body. It was coming home. Everything else could wait, fear and uncertainty had no place in their bed. Tomorrow was soon enough to face the peril awaiting them in the guise of friend and foe.

CHAPTER 24

AMORA MEDINA-JACKYL

A soft hand rested on her shoulder, and Amora turned her head to glance up at her smiling mate. She wrapped her arm around Lark's waist and pulled the woman down on her lap. Nuzzling the side of Lark's throat, she smirked as her mate shivered and burrowed closer. They both brought their attention to the people sitting at the table. Ripper sat to her left with Tasha beside him, Nicolette on her right and Meadow was beside her.

Fuck, it had all changed in so short a time, Amora never thought she would see any of her siblings again. She had a family again, and she couldn't discount Seamus' pack. They were family as well, and blood didn't always make a family.

Lark held her tight, it was all somewhat surreal, and she didn't know how to handle it. Part of her was waiting to wake up, back in the cell, starved and desperate. She didn't want to discover this life she'd made was only a madness-induced hallucination. The events of the last couple months a dream, a respite from Hell.

"Hey." Gentle fingertips lovingly stroked her cheek drawing her attention.

"Don't start, Lark."

"Who said I was going to start anything?"

A wicked grin and eyes dancing with amusement made Amora's smirk. Her tongue darted out and stroked over Lark's quickened pulse.

"I know you too well, Lark." A growl rumbled in her chest as she shifted her mate on her lap, slender fingers palming the lush curves of Lark's ass.

"Am I so easy to read after only a year and a half?"

Amora slid her hand lower until she could slip between Lark's thighs from behind.

A throat clearing caused her brow to arch as she shot her son a scathing look. "Can we have our first family meal without you trying to molest my stepmother at the fu—" Amora snorted as Ripper censored himself. "Table?"

"Isn't that sweet, trying to act like a grownup." A gravelly chuckle was muffled by Lark's soft hair as she glanced with amusement at her son.

"Fuck you, Amora. I'm more mature than you are." She nearly choked as she laughed.

"Kid, works better if you don't pout. Meadow doesn't sulk as much as you." Nico slumped casually in her chair, but even with her relaxed posture Amora could tell her sister was alert. Nico was prepared for any sign of danger and able to react without thought. The darkness that was haunting her sister's gaze tempered Amora's contentment of their first family dinner.

"Been in the family a few weeks and you're already in competition for Queen Bitch with Amora." Slender shoulders shrugged as a brow arched as Ripper and Nico faced off across the expanse of the table.

"Ripper!" Tasha's elbow found Ripper's ribs, and he turned to glare at her while rubbing the spot.

"What, baby? Damn, I'm gonna choke on the estrogen floating around this place." His eyes widened.

"You fucked up now, Son."

Amora relaxed back to watch the fireworks and cuddled her mate to her chest. Lark turned her head, and soft lips nibbled at her mouth. High-pitched giggles came from her right as she opened her eyes to find Meadow standing beside them. She snaked her arm around her daughter and pulled her up to sit on her lap as well.

"Does dinner always come with a show?" Epoch's weirdly husky voice broke them apart.

"Just sit over there, you little perv. How the hell did you get an invite to dinner?"

"Lark was sweet enough to ask me." Epoch wiggled in his chair and turned an almost shy glance in Lark's direction.

Aw, fuck no, that wasn't happening. Amora turned her head to meet Lark's innocent gaze and caught the flutter of lashes.

"We are not adopting him," Amora snarled. "And I don't think he particularly looks at you like a mother-figure."

"But, Amora, he's sweet, just a bit misunderstood and we already discussed that his choice of menu items wasn't acceptable here. See…" Lark pointed to Epoch. "I made him cookies."

Somewhere on the fringes of her mind, she heard the quiet argument going on between Ripper and Tasha, but right now she needed to prevent a new adoption.

"Ada even tried some raw meat, but he's better with cookies until he gets home."

"Ada, don't encourage your Mother."

"It's not my fault the woman is insane. She thinks you're perfect, why not think some cannibalistic Ghoul is sweet and misunderstood." Ada plopped down in her seat.

They didn't see enough of their oldest adopted daughter. Ada's travels were more about outrunning her past than to see new sights and have once in a lifetime adventures. One day she hoped, like Ripper, Ada would come home, but she wouldn't push.

"I can be sweet." Epoch pouted from his end of the table.

"I'm sure you can, honey."

Epoch seemed to turn pink at the endearment and batted his lashes.

"Epoch, I will kill you."

"What I do?"

"You know what you did. Keep it in your pants."

"Everyone wants me to keep it in my pants. I'm almost a thousand years old, damn it. I don't want to keep it in my pants."

"This is the dinner table, Epoch, you do that somewhere private," Lark chided Epoch.

"Yes, ma'am."

He went silent and nibbled on cookies and sipped his milk.

"Oh fuck, what the hell is going on here?"

When had her family turned into some dysfunctional clusterfuck? Ghouls, humans, vampires, and seers at the family dinner table. Her extended family just seemed to get weirder every year.

"Momma Mora, Ripper's in trouble." The little girl spoke in a stage whisper.

"Yes, he is, but he'll learn quickly to watch his tongue." Soft brown curls bounced as she nodded like she understood. The effects of Meadow's kidnapping and imprisonment by Angelus had faded. Her happy, yet quiet adopted daughter was back to normal. This was what she had fought through the insanity for, a dream she'd thought unattainable, but still wanted.

"Oh, is that right? Maybe you can sleep on the couch from now on, so you don't choke on the estrogen from your daughter and me."

"Tasha, don't be mean." Her son protested and pouted as he tried to give Tasha his most pathetic look.

"How did you even talk that female out of her panties?" Nico asked.

Amora snickered as Ripper flipped Nico off. "I have an irresistible charm, Nico."

"Yeah," Amora observed as Nico turned her attention to Tasha. "I bet I can be even more charming than you." Nico flicked her tongue over her fang and winked at a blushing Tasha.

Ripper's face turned red, and his eyes narrowed. "Nico, is there a mate waiting for you at home?"

A veil fell across Nico's expression, and a chill filled the air.

"I don't have time for mates. My job doesn't allow for it." Nico's tone showed that was all the information she was going to give.

Again, a sadness lingered beneath the surface. Too much remained unspoken, no sharing of pasts aside from the obvious reality of Angelus. Lark must have sensed Amora's unease, and a soft hand stroked her cheek. Her mate was trying to soothe the tangle of dark emotions always existing beneath the surface.

Amora smiled at Lark and nodded as she searched for safer topics. "What is that again? Ripper said he found you fighting in a warehouse."

"That was purely for fun." She waited as the silence lengthened until shoulders squared. "I'm a bounty hunter, preternatural clients mostly, but I occasionally take on a job from a human."

"Run your own agency?" She and Nico had more in common than she anticipated, she hoped they didn't share parts too painful to bear.

"Unofficially. Demon Bounty Agency. I work out of my car and motel room."

"Why don't you settle here for opening an office. Now that I'm retired, I have a few contacts that could use your services."

"I don't like staying in one place too long." Her sister's jaw ticked as back teeth clenched.

"We all have secrets, Nico, ones we'll never escape, but here you have a family to watch your back. You don't have to make a decision now, just think about it. Besides, I just met you. I'd hate to let you go." The only response she received was a stiff nod.

A heaviness descended around the table. She had her sister back, the sister she'd thought dead long ago. Still, there seemed to be something off, missing. Naomi was dead, yet that didn't mean the others didn't survive. Bram, maybe even their baby brother not yet born, although, Amora didn't want to wish for things that wouldn't happen, she couldn't let it rest—not yet anyway.

"Ma?"

Ripper called her name, and she met his concerned gaze. Her eyes skittered down the remaining empty chairs; her arms tightened around her mate and Meadow. Nodding her head, she sat straighter in her chair at the head of the table.

"We find them, dead or alive."

"No one gets left behind."

Out of the corner of her eye, she watched Ripper wrap Tasha in his arms, but Nico remained stiff and alone. Ada chose to leave the table and Epoch focused on his plate.

Meadow wiggled out from under Amora's arm, and her tiny feet pounded against the floor until she stopped beside Nico's chair. A brief flash of panic widened her sister's eyes as Meadow climbed onto the woman's lap.

There was a rigidity to Nico's movements as she twined her arms around Meadow. Affection and trust weren't an ingrained trait. Too many years spent with your back to a wall, waiting for an attack. It's why she needed to keep her sister close.

No one gets left behind, it had been Ripper and her motto for years, but it was more than the two of them now. Lark, Meadow, Tasha and Nico, Ada, even a grandchild on the way joined into the dysfunction that was Ripper and Amora.

Amora had to make Nico understand.

A broken, husky sound drew her attention, and she looked into fiery black eyes. "No one gets left behind." Nico nodded and turned her gaze away.

Amora's body eased as a wave of peace came over her, muscled relaxed as she let the darkness go and tucked Lark closer. "I love you."

"I love you too." Gentle fingertips stroked along exposed scars. This was what she had nearly sold her soul for, vengeance had brought her contentment, but still, there was so much more to come.

EPILOGUE

ANGELUS

$\mathcal{M}$illennia had passed since he had ascended from the primordial depths. Angelus Kali felt his time running out, his pathetic son and grandson closing in. The Medina-Jackyl clan was growing in ranks and strength, so much awaited them. He needed to destroy them before they actually learned the power they possessed. Ripper, the half-breed, his power grew by the day as that whore of his bred the bastard child. That bitch Seer that had escaped him. He growled as his demon shimmered under the surface.

Fingers carded through his black mane of hair and he stiffened as he sensed he was no longer alone.

"Master?"

Cecil's voice broke through Angelus' thoughts as he gazed into the leaping flames in the hearth. Rage seethed pushing aside the pain as his body slowly pieced itself back together. Gauze encircled his head covering the now empty eye socket where claws had dug and pierced his eye, ripped his flesh.

"What is it?" he growled at his servant.

"I have the information you requested." A snarl tugged at the corners of his mouth.

"Leave it and get out." He ordered as he surged from the leather chair and his usually dominant form moved with stuttered movements. The battle between Ripper and himself caused more damage than it should have.

Angelus felt as if he dwelled in the bottom of an hourglass, each speck of sand flowed in slow motion building and threatening to suffocate him beneath the minuscule weight.

Cecil didn't speak, merely dropped the files on the desk and backed out of Angelus' study quickly. The sniveling weakling allegiance rested elsewhere, loyalty silently pledged to his bastard grandson. He could make Cecil beg to be released in the most agonizing ways, yet the male still served a purpose, even Cecil didn't understand.

The plan was precise, prophesized in perfect detail, but he knew everything could change at any moment. Paths diverged, free will and fate, nothing was absolute not even so-called prophecies. It was up to him to make sure the pawns moved and that the Queen died and the King sacrificed himself.

He stepped behind his desk, eased into his chair and stroked scarred fingertips along the edges of the folders. Revelations of nightmares existed within, everything he needed to break his greatest enemies slowly. They must never band together. The Order was his strongest weapon, and the tainted blood would flow.

Family turning against one another, betrayal is how every great war began. Although battles remained, the war would come soon enough. He opened the first folder; one narrowed eye scanned the information contained inside.

Oh, how he longed to destroy them, forget about the plan and forge ahead. It would all happen in due time. Everything needed to happen on a strict timetable. Death was too easy and quick, descents into madness and betrayal those were the things that lingered. He wanted them to suffer, and Angelus had the perfect tools for that.

He sneered as he relaxed back in his chair and darted a glance to a darkened corner as he felt the air in the room displace.

"You summoned me?" The voice an inhuman growl as a massive cloaked formed stepped forward.

"Is everything in place?"

Angelus' fingers formed a steeple as he put the tips under his chin.

"It is as it should be, events are in motion, and all players are where they belong. May I speak freely, Master?"

"Of course, you are my most trusted advisor."

"Do you believe this is a sensible plan, Kali? This is a dangerous game you've started. If all the players are allowed to meet, you will have no chance of victory. All your effort will be for naught."

"To do what needs to be done, all the pieces must be on the board, Lucien. This game was set in motion long ago. I kept all the players separate as it was meant to be, now, they must all converge at just the right times."

"I still find it unwise, some of the players are stronger than even you have anticipated."

The demon lowered his head in a show of submission, but Angelus knew that Lucien's respect was false.

"Have I not promised you the reward you most want to possess?" A flash of sharp, white teeth was revealed by what he knew was a vicious smile.

Angelus was well aware everyone had their vice, and no one was immune—everyone had a price. Whatever base need his followers, and the ones loyal to him, were provided for, Lucien was no different. He was weak, obsessed with one thing. But his sadistic streak craved only one victim, and Angelus promised him to Lucien as soon as he succeeded.

"To taste the sweetness of that flesh once more." A lust-filled growl followed the words. "No one's screams and fear were ever as beautiful...I want to trace my marks once more."

The demon disgusted him. "Yes, but there is much to do before that can happen. Their search will continue, and I need you to lurk in the shadows until they amass all the pawns."

"It will be done, Master Kali. I merely hope that your arrogance doesn't make you careless."

Angelus brought his fist down on the desk heavily and narrowed his eye as Lucien bowed. "You will watch your tongue, or I will take great pleasure in carving it from your mouth."

"My apologies."

Lucien's respectful bow was even an insult. He doubted he would be able to trust the demon much longer, yet he hoped Lucien had served his purpose before he had to do away with him.

"Get out."

Lucien spun, his cloak billowing as he disappeared in a haze of black smoke.

That demon would require more vigilance, enemies existed in his numbers, and they all conspired if not with his enemies but for them. Disloyalty was effortless among demons and other creatures, in the end, the reality was everyone for themselves. He separated the folders, placed them in order and studied the names on each one.

First to be sacrificed, Nicolette, the next in line for matriarch of the Jackyl clan. So much pain awaited, she thought her past was painful, yet she had no idea the Hell he had planned for her. He growled as an evil smirk pulled at his lips, and he picked up her file.

Eye scanned the last three hundred years of her life. Every vile torture she was subjected to, each creature that used and discarded her and the apparitions still afflicting her.

Knowledge was power, especially when that familiarity foretold the fears. It was a recipe for madness in the making, and he would break them all without mercy. But first, he would allow them their silly dreams before he ripped them apart.

He closed his eye, pictured the place he needed to be and felt the crackle in the air, the prickle beneath his skin before he opened his eye. "Dominic."

"I would be lying if I said it was a pleasant surprise." Dominic took a seat in one of the two chairs in front of the hearth.

Angelus strode across the room to take the empty chair and crossed his legs. He took long moments to study the decaying demon. To be honest, he grew tired of Dominic, his treachery and disrespect, unfortunately, no one else was as gifted as Dominic.

"We have been acquainted far too long for petty little lies. You have been quite busy."

"From what I have gleaned, you have as well. What do you want, Kali?"

"Do you believe your interference will change anything? You are merely wasting your time."

"I find I have nothing but time, Kali, as you can see." Angelus watched the ancient male motion around the stone chamber. "You made quite certain I'd never leave this room, and I do love my small amusements."

"What do you gain from assisting them? You were to possess the child, train one of the most powerful seers to be born. It would've been a great honor."

"For you, possibly. I won't mindlessly assist you in your plans. I'm also aware of your inability to do away with me. I'm beneficial to this project of yours, and I cannot wait to witness your fall due to your arrogance. You cannot win, no matter what has been foretold, the end will always be the same.

"Amora is too powerful, as are the rest of the enemies you plot against with this scheme. Kali, you will fail, you grow weaker every day and sooner rather than later you will expire. Your grandson will ascend." Angelus clenched his teeth as Dominic's eyes fell on the bandage and the male chuckled.

"Your existence today is only allowed since Ripper is not yet ready to take your place. You subsist on borrowed time. I must admire Amora's son for allowing you to live. I was unaware that the vamp instilled mercy in her offspring."

"You push too hard, Dominic, and I will forget about your usefulness."

"You will do no such thing, and I will assist your enemy at every turn. I may be restricted from informing them of every detail, but I can give them all the clues they need. There is always a way, Kali. You have forgotten the fragility of your existence. Arrogance, Kali, has made you blind. You have endured too long in the position of Soul Collector."

Angelus observed the male as he leaned forward in his chair, Dominic sneered at him, and amusement lit up his eyes.

"Kali, you will fail, it is written, and no matter how you try to mold the future to fit your expectations, it doesn't change what is destined to come. I will watch your fall and celebrate it."

Angelus swept his hand through the air. Dominic surged backward in his chair, and the smile on the male's face infuriated him. "You're wrong, they will all die, just as it should've been, and I won't stop until I have destroyed their line, all of them!"

"No, you're wrong, Angelus. You should have killed Amora along with the rest of her family. Your need for a weapon—a bragging right sealed your fate as much as it did hers. Forces will be combined. They will discover your trickery. Like you tried with Arian, Samuel, and Helena, history will repeat itself, but this time, you won't be counting coups."

Releasing the male, he returned to his home and cleared the desk with an angry arc of his arm. Papers fluttered to the ground as he pounded his fist on his desk, listening to the wood crack and give under the force. Their deaths would happen, failure wasn't an option, and all would die, the line and their allies.

Angelus calmed himself as he envisioned the carnage and completion of a plan centuries in the making. Finally, he would succeed, patience was key—he just needed to be patient. "All in due time."

THE END

ABOUT THE AUTHOR

J.M. Dabney is a multi-genre author who writes mainly LGBT romance and fiction. She lives with a constant diverse cast of characters in her head. No matter their size, shape, race, etc. she lives for one purpose alone, and that's to make sure she does them justice and give them the happily ever after they deserve. J.M. is dysfunction at its finest and she makes sure her characters are a beautiful kaleidoscope of crazy. There is nothing more she wants from telling her stories than to show that no matter the package the characters come in or the damage their pasts have done, that love is love. That normal is never normal and sometimes the so-called broken can still be amazing.

www.ingramcontent.com/pod-product-compliance
Lightning Source LLC
Chambersburg PA
CBHW060152130626
46556CB00006B/2609